THE DEVIL STOPPED

BY

A NOVEL

Sha-shonda Porter

F.I.R.E.

ISBN: 0988325500

ISBN-13: 978-0-9883255-0-0

The devil might stop by, but he can't stay here!

Thanks to all of you who ever thought I could accomplish great things, and vowed to love me even if I did not.

A great many thanks to all of the teachers and professors who have encouraged me and who have helped me to shape my vision and thoughts.

Finally, I offer much gratitude to my parents, Curtis and Virgie Porter.

The sun glared, dominoes slammed, men cursed, and two women fought in the middle of the street, but we just kept on jumping.

> Little girl, little girl turn around.
> Little girl, little girl touch the ground.
> Little girl, little girl fly the plane.
> Little girl, little girl spell your name.
> R-U-T-H-I

"Ruthie!" My mother's voice chimed in over Cyndi's just when she was about to shout the final E of my name.

"Ruthie, time for you to come in." Mom was standing on the steps leading up to the doorway of our small apartment.

On one of the sunniest summer days that Chicago has ever seen, I have to go in two hours before the sun even thinks about going down. Ten years old and I can't even stay out until sunset. I don't think I'll make a fuss today though. Cyndi talked me into trying that last week, and it landed me a good whoopin'.

"You always gotta go in early. You gotta go study your Bible school lesson don't ya Ruthie?"

Cyndi didn't wait for me to answer. I really don't know why she acts like she's asking a question. She always talks really fast, like she's in a hurry or something. She rested on the stoop in front of her apartment building. Everybody always tells her how pretty she is. Her mom says they are part Cherokee Indian. Cyndi sat there with her hands supporting her chin.

"My momma says you gonna be messed up in the head with all that religious carrying on," Cyndi said in her miss smarty-pants, know everything tone of voice. Her hazel eyes always looked like she was doing devilment, but I knew she didn't mean any harm. Hazel. What kind of color is hazel? When I first met Cyndi, I told her that I liked her light brown eyes. That's what they are. Light brown with flecks of gold. But she rolled her light brown and gold eyes and told me that her eyes were hazel, and that I should learn my colors. Now, she and her hazel eyes sat there on her stoop judging me.

"Being crazy is better than going to hell."

I didn't believe it but it was the only thing I could think of to say. I was just trying to shut Cyndi up. If I had time to sit and think about it for a while, I could have come up with something better. With that, I turned and began to walk as fast as I could towards my doorway.

I swept past my mom and headed straight down the narrow hall to the back of the apartment. The almost-yellow wallpaper had new air creases each day. It was as if it had decided that it needed to escape our neighborhood, our home. Little-by-little, it puffed itself up, and at just the right moment, it would run. It allowed its bright yellow color to fade to almost-yellow, and what used to be small white flowers with green leaves were hardly noticeable any more. It was becoming less conspicuous. C-O-N-S-P-. I couldn't remember how to spell it, but it was on my spelling list last year. I know that I'd memorized it because I got 100s on all of my spelling tests. The wallpaper was becoming less conspicuous, so when it was all gone, nobody would even notice. I was glad that it was planning its escape. I liked to run my hands along the air creases and feel the difference between the smooth and raised wallpaper. I wanted to help it, to tear away small pieces. I started in the bottom corners where Mama wouldn't notice.

Before I could make it to the bedroom door, she yelled. "Ruthie, get cleaned up for supper and get your books out so you can study when we're done eating." I moved my lips along with her words. She gave the same orders every day.

Cyndi was right, I probably will be crazy. I feel like I am half-way there already. Especially with the dreams. She'd say I was crazy for sure if I told her how sometimes I just knew stuff before it even happened. It's sort of like Ezekial or John or something. Like maybe God tells me, but I just know. Ten and crazy.

"Ruthie, did you hear me?" Mama said again.

"Yes ma'am." I am pretty sure that no other ten year old on this earth has read as many verses as me. It wouldn't do any good to tell her that I didn't want to study, that's like talking to a wall and sitting there waiting for an answer. The rule is that as long as you are in this house, you will study the gospel and you will govern yourself accordingly. That's Father's rule, and of course whatever Father says is law. He always says, we are not going to have the devil living in this house. He may stop by, but he won't stay long.

By the time I lay down on my bed, my face was wet with tears. Nothing was really wrong, it just wasn't right. There was a pressing from the bottom of my neck to the center of my chest. It was like an invisible hand bearing down on me that caused the tears to spill from my eyes for at least five minutes.

When I heard the front door slam, I jumped up and raced to the restroom to wash up. I washed as hard and as fast as I could.

"Don't make Father angry. Ruthie don't make Father angry." Barely moving my lips, I mumbled the words to myself in the mirror. With water as hot as I could stand, I scrubbed, removing any trace of the tears that had somehow escaped from my eyes.

Turning to walk out, the reflection of my uncontrollable plaits in the mirror grabbed my attention. Fear bounced from my heart to my throat and then back again. Mom always kept the brush in the medicine cabinet. I opened the mirrored door and took the brush. With the mirror as my witness, I brushed and brushed. Stroke after stroke was time wasted. I put one plait down, another popped up. It was hopeless. Mama could put grease and water on her coal black, water-wavy hair and it would lay down straight, but not mine. My hair was not like mama's, not much was.

She was tall and pretty. Some of the ladies on the block called her a half-breed or high yellow because she was light-skinned. Men were always drinking her up with their eyes. When she walked down the street, everybody stared, both men and women.

Folks always say I look like Father had me all by his self. And mostly, they are right. I am darker than most and I got his broad nose and kinky hair. My eyes bug out and my teeth are big enough to fill any grown-up's mouth. I guess I don't make a very good picture.

I hurried out of the bathroom towards the kitchen. As I turned the corner, I barely missed bumping into Father. His dark brown suit jacket was thrown over his shoulder and the top two buttons of his off-white shirt were undone along with his tie. His coal-black conked hair was parted on the left side and slicked down with pomade.

Sometimes it's hard to tell the hustlers from the preachers. They all kinda remind you of one another, the way they strut around all fancied up. They are silent enemy partners with the same goal, to save. If they save you from your demons, then you are indebted to them. You owe them, you are at their mercy. To cook their meals, buy their jewels, make their babies, whatever. All for a little salvation.

"Ruthie, look where you're going."

I jumped and held my breath.

"Yes sir. Good evening sir," I mumbled, looking down at his freshly shined black Stacy Adams. He had spent most of one of his paychecks to get those shoes. Said he had to have them because you can tell a man of good standing by the shoes that he wears. He can't go sitting in a pulpit looking any kind of way. That's the reason he gave to mama when there wasn't enough money left to cover all the bills. She'd had to ask Ms. Dora to lend her the money.

"He ain't been preachin' but a hot minute and he gon' go and spend up ya'll rent on some damned shoes?" Ms. Dora sat on the steps in front of our building. At first, she was trying to make mama feel better about having to borrow rent money, now she seemed mad.

"Dora, you know I'll pay you back" mama sounded like a little girl compared to the fullness of Ms. Dora's voice.

"Ain't 'bout that. You ought not be havin' to borrow. He take his black ass to work instead of hangin' round up there at that church…" I loved listening to Ms. Dora. She was in Chicago, "by way of Georgia," as she'd say. She sang all of her words, adding an extra syllable to each of them.

"Dora, I told you they cut him to part time. They won't give him but three days a week over at the plant." Had it been anyone else cursing the way Ms. Dora was, mama would have pronounced them as ignorant, but she didn't look down on Ms. Dora's cursing like she did others.

"Yeah, well, still." Ms. Dora and mama sat there for a minute, quiet. I kicked the ball a little closer to the steps, just in case they started whispering. I had only been playing with the ball so that I could hear what they were saying. This was one of those times that I was happy that I had to stay in the yard, which was nothing but a small patch of grass about four steps long and four steps wide.

Ms. Dora looked like the woman from that movie, *Imitation of Life*; the mother, not the pretty one. Mama looked like the pretty one. Even when she was asking for money, she looked like she could've been rich with her straight back and long neck. Ms. Dora always looked tired, but she always kept money.

"I don't know why ya'll yaller gals always latch on to these no-good, black niggers anyhow. You oughta switch that yaller tail over to the north side and get you one of them suit-wearing, young, white mens that don't mind payin' for a little black cat." Ms. Dora laughed like only she could, down from somewhere deep inside her belly. She slapped her knee, threw her head back, and opened her mouth wide so that the laugh could come out strong. Why would a white man pay for a black cat? I thought hard about it. Black cats are bad luck and we don't have one to sell anyway.

A slight wind stirred up hot air and the smell of old garbage. Flies buzzed around the trashcans that had been sitting along the edges of the sidewalk for the last three days. Trashcans lined our whole street. Most of them overflowed, spilling empty boxes and cartons, broken bottles, wadded paper, table scraps, and dirty diapers into the streets. Cyndi and I had counted the trashcans earlier that day before lunch; there were twenty-seven of them. Starting at my house, take seven giant steps and then you would be at the next set of trashcans. Seven more giant steps, and you would be at the next set. You could do this all the way down the block. Sometimes it was really five or six giant steps, but we made our steps smaller because seven was Cyndi's lucky number.

"Dora, you ought to be ashamed of yourself." Mama tried to look mad and serious at the same time, but I could tell that she really wasn't. "Ruthie what are you looking at?" Mama snapped. "I know you are not eavesdropping on grownup conversation." She squinted her eyes and clinched her thin lips together, a sign of trouble.

"No ma'am." I lowered my chin to my chest. I had gotten so busy listening that I had forgotten to act like I was playing with the ball. Instead, I had been looking straight into their faces.

"Don't you lie to me girl! Get on in the house!"

"'Scuse me Ms. Dora," I mumbled as I walked between her and mama, up the steps, to the front door.

"Ruthie! Where is your mind at girl?" Father's voice shook me. Looking at his shoes, I'd gotten lost in my thoughts and forgotten that I was still standing in his way. Without taking my eyes off his black Stacy Adams, I pressed myself up against the hallway wall to let him by.

The smell of mama's fried chicken slapped me in the face as I rounded the corner into the kitchen. Fried chicken, mashed potatoes, black-eyed peas and cornbread all arranged at the center of the table.

"Ruthie, get the glasses out of the cabinet and pour everyone some water."

Never even turning to see whether it was me, Mama gave orders from the sink. Taking out three glasses and the ice, I did just as I was told.

"What's got you moving so slowly, girl? Hurry on over and set those glasses down, so we can have dinner." Whenever Father was around, Mama did everything quickly and wanted me to do the same.

Me and Mama sat at the table saying nothing. Sometimes it seemed like Father just wanted to see how long he could make us wait. Nothing else to do, I fidgeted with my hands underneath the table, checking to make sure that there wasn't any trace of dirt underneath my fingernails.

"Ruthie, quit fidgeting," mom said impatiently, but quietly.

"I'm hungry," was the only thing that I felt safe enough to say.

"Oh hush now, your dad will be in soon."

She said that at least four more times before he came in. Had it been me taking so long, she would have called and threatened to come speed me up with the belt, but with Father she was nothing but a mouse. Now, in only his pants and white undershirt, he sat down without a word to anyone and mumbled a prayer over the food. He always said the prayers. Said it's his duty because he's the head of this household and responsible for all that goes on in it. Always the same prayer too.

"God, we would like to thank you for all that you have set before us today. We know that we may not have everything that we want, but you have surely given us everything that we need. May everything here be pleasing in your sight. In the name of Jesus we pray. Amen."

Sometimes, I wonder if God gets tired of hearing the same thing day in and day out. If he doesn't, I sure do. Without looking up, Father fixed his plate. When he started to eat, mom and I fixed ours. The clanging of forks against the plates was loud. Then, without a word ever being said, dinner was finally over.

Lying on my bed, I opened my Bible and Sunday school guide. The small yellow daisies on the sheet that mama uses to separate my side of the room from her and Father's, seem out of place. This Sunday we would talk about the Ten Commandments. I'd read this at least a hundred times before, but I figured I better read it again because Sister Pearl would surely call on me to answer questions. It never failed. She calls on me every Sunday.

I wondered what Cyndi is doing right now. Or any other normal kid for that matter. I wondered what it would be like to have someone to stay over with me. We could stay up late into the night and play games and tell secrets. We could imagine that we were both queens all dressed up in fancy dresses and robes with diamond rings on every finger. Maybe we would just be two girlfriends that lived next door to one another with our fancy, doctor husbands. We would have our own cars and fur coats and diamond rings. I might become a teacher if I got bored. Or maybe, I would just travel around the world instead. Yes, I would go on vacation even if my fancy, doctor husband couldn't go. He would say, "Enjoy yourself darling," as he handed me a million dollars. He would always call me darling. Darling. And he would kiss the back of my hand like they do in the movies.

"I'll be back later," I heard Father say as his footsteps seemed to be going towards the front door.

"Where are you going, Herbert?"

I could barely hear Mama ask the question above the quiet whine of the front door opening.

"I said, I will be back later. Ain't that enough for you?"

Father's voice was now raised to that familiar, I am MAN tone.

"I would just like to know where you are going. It's late," Mama's voice squeaked.

The door slammed, but the quick and heavy footsteps had to be Father's. Next there was some yelling, and then I heard some things falling or being thrown. Then, there were some dull sounds.

"Stop Herbert, please." Mama pleaded beneath her sobs. "I'm sorry. I'm sorry."

I could hear his blows landing on her body.

"It hurts, Herbert. Stop, please stop. I'm sorry." Mama whimpered just like the time when she had gotten on her knees, cupped her hands like she was praying to him, and begged Father not to hit her.

After a while everything got pretty quiet. The only thing worse than the noise is the quiet. At least when there is noise, I can tell what is going on, but when it's quiet I don't really know what to expect. Finally, the front door opened and slammed again and all that was left was Mama's muffled crying. I lay on my back, as still as possible, hoping to disappear or just float up to heaven. Looking up at the ceiling, I tried not to move, I didn't want to make any sound. Sometimes I held my breath, because it seemed like my breathing was as loud as the yelling. I tried to close my eyes, but each time that I tried, they'd sting from the heat of the tears I promised myself I would not let fall. I just lay there letting the speech that Father would give me, if he came home early enough, run through my mind. He would start by asking if I understood what had happened. Then, he would tell me how it wasn't his fault, how sometimes Mama got out of her place and pushed him too far. How it was just the devil, the way that she talked to him and made him angry. Then we would have to pray so that the devil's spirit would have to flee. And when we finished praying, he would say, the devil may stop by, but he sure can't stay here. Then he would make sure that I understood that our home is private, and it would be the devil for me to say anything to anyone.

Sugar pie honey bunch, Uncle Byrd was back again. He showed up last night with nothing but a small suitcase and his record player. You know that I love you. I can't help myself, I love you and nobody else. The Temptations could have been standing right there in the living room. The record player was blaring, but I could still hear Uncle Byrd jiving and sliding across the floor. The music was so exciting, not like the gospel that played from our window radio when Mama cleaned house on Saturday mornings. Until I could catch myself, my hips and shoulders were swinging with the beat. I rounded the corner into the living room and was greeted by a huge white-toothed smile.

Uncle Byrd was tall and slender. Unlike most of the other men around our neighborhood, he always looked and smelled good. His shirt was always tucked inside pressed pants that fit just right. Him and Father favored a lot, but they were as different as night and day. Just like Father, Uncle Byrd was darker than midnight, but there were no traces of facial hair on his smooth skin.

Whenever Uncle Byrd stepped into a room, it was as if the lights came on. Like before he got there, the lights had been off and you didn't know it. Uncle Byrd was always excited about something or other. He always had some part of a plan to go on about.

No matter what the subject, a story was always interesting when he told it. He was Father's only brother, but if Father had more than one, Uncle Byrd definitely would not have been his favorite.

"Baby girl, ain't nothing better for the soul than a good song."

He crooned as he trotted across the floor gyrating and sweating.

"This is where it's at right here. I ain't got time to be sittin' around listening to other folks sang about their problems. Talkin' bout their woman done left 'em, took the kids, the car, and the dog. Hell, baby girl, I got enough worries of my own. Ain't tryin' to hear nobody else's."

Uncle Byrd had spirit like nobody else had spirit. The church ladies didn't have anything on him.

When I heard knocking at the front door, I froze. I was sure that it would be someone standing there, pointing their finger. Telling me, you know better than listening to that devil's music, as if I had some choice in the matter.

"Hey, baby girl. That's probably my lady friend."

Uncle Byrd ran over to the record player, took off the Four Tops and put on Percy Sledge.

<u>When a man loves a woman…</u>

"Now here," he said reaching down into his front pocket and pulling out twenty-five cents. "Why don't you run down to the corner market and get yourself something good."

"What about Cyndi? She'll want something. You know, Father doesn't let me walk down there by myself, so she'll have to go too." I added the last part because I knew this would be one of those visits that Uncle Byrd would want to keep secret.

"Awright baby girl. Here's another quarter. Get something for Cyndi, too. Get on now and don't walk too fast, it's hot out there."

Mama and Father had gone to mid-day prayer meeting and wouldn't be back for another couple of hours. He always let her go to mid-day prayer. It made him look good for his wife to come along with him. It was the night-time prayer meetings that she wasn't allowed to attend. Father said it was men only. Praying and handling church business. They don't need any women mixed up in church business. I didn't know of anyone else's Father going to prayer meeting on Friday and Saturday nights. I guess Father was more dedicated, since Reverend Johansen licensed him to preach. He sat in the pulpit on Sundays and even preached once a month. Reverend Johansen didn't share his pulpit much, but he said Father had a special gift.

I opened the door and stepped outside. The damp heat made it hard to take a deep breath. Passing by Uncle Byrd's lady friend, I realized it was Jeanie from across the street. She was Ms. Dora's middle daughter. She had her fifteenth birthday party last week, but with her make-up and short skirts she always seemed older. One day when Ms. Dora was over for coffee, she told mama that Jeanie was already ''bout used up.'

Jeanie lowered her eyes when I looked at her bright red lips. She was pretty. I almost smiled at her, but she looked away. Head down, she walked inside to Uncle Byrd. Why had I even thought she would want to smile at me? She's older and cool and pretty.

Normally, there would be boys playing ball in the streets, women standing around sharing the latest gossip, and men at rickety homemade tables playing dominoes or some other game that required a lot of drinking and cussing. But today, there were only three boys outside and they looked like the sun had robbed them and left them for dead. There was no one laying in the alley or sitting on the hood of the car that had not moved since I could remember. None of the girls that usually ignored me or teased me about my hair and bony knees were out playing hopscotch. Some folks looked out of their windows, but that was as close to outside as they were coming. I could hear the box fans sitting in the windows, straining to keep pulling.

Climbing the three flights of stairs to get to Cyndi's door, I decided on ice cream. I would definitely buy ice cream.

The smell of pinto beans and pee was strong. The pinto beans had a little pork fat in them, but it was mostly pee that I smelled. Cyndi's building always had folks hanging around in the hallways and stairwells, and if they couldn't make it to the bathroom, they would just pee right there where they were. With my hands down by my side, I made sure not to get any of the stairway gunk on myself.

I knew the door was probably unlocked, but I knocked anyway.

"What?" Cyndi's mom called, interrupting my thoughts of ice cream, pinto beans, and pee.

Inching the door open, "It's me, Ruthie," I told her as I stuck my head inside.

"What you creepin' for? Come on in here." Ms. Hawkins was sprawled out on the couch. "Child, what are you doing out in this heat?" Staring at me with glassy eyes, she scratched her forearm and then her thigh. Her long wavy hair hung loosely, not in the usual knot on top of her head. Ms. Hawkins' home-cut bangs stood straight up in the air as proof that she had been sitting face forward in front of the fan in the window.

"Does your mama know you're out here? Come on in." Just like Cyndi. She always sounded like she was asking a question, but she never gave you time to answer.

When I told Cyndi what had happened with Uncle Byrd, she wanted to go peek through the window since I lived on the ground floor. A little boost, an over-turned wagon, or a stepping stool someone had tossed out, that's all we would really need to get a good peek.

"We will do no such devilment. Do you want ice cream or not?" I hadn't given Cyndi any other options. I enjoyed the rare occasions when I had more say so than Cyndi. She always chose the games, where we would go, what we would do, and who we would like. But, I had the money, and I had already decided on ice cream. Cyndi would just have to go along with what I'd decided. I walked more quickly, so that Cyndi would either have to hurry to catch up or let me lead her.

"Well, of course I want ice cream. What kind of question is that? I just thought we'd have a little fun first. You're so square Ruthie. Just an old fuddy duddy." Cyndi went from subject-to-subject as we headed towards the corner. "You say your mama AND your daddy at prayer meeting?"

"Yes, you know that. Why would you ask a silly question like that, when I just told you?" Sometimes Cyndi's never-ending jabbering frustrated me.

"Well, it ain't so silly. My mama say he just be foolin' your mama talking about he's going to prayer meeting. She say he be praying alright. Making Sister Jesse say 'hallelujah!'"

"Shut up Cyndi, you don't know anything about being respectful."

I wasn't really sure what Cyndi was talking about, but by the tone in her voice and the way she waved her hands, I was sure that it was disrespectful, and I was ashamed. "Two ice cream cones please," I said to the old, leathery white face.

"**M**an, they don't give a damn about you!"

Sitting on the hard wood floor, I pretended not to hear Uncle Byrd's cuss word. With my back propped against the couch, I kept on looking at the words in my book, hoping I wouldn't be sent to the bedroom.

"Byrd, you know I don't allow that swearing in my house. You are not at some joint with your low-life partners."

"Okay, whatever, but I get tired of black folks believing everything that white folks tell 'em." Uncle Byrd's voice was shaking and much louder now. "We have got to take a stand, else we gonna be living in these same funky conditions forever."

"So now my house isn't good enough for you?" Father left the couch that had been pushed against the wall to make room for Uncle Byrd's pallet, and crossed the room to his glass of water on the kitchen cabinet. Taking a sip, he crumbled up the red paper that Uncle Byrd had given him and threw it into the trashcan. "It was good enough two weeks ago when you didn't have anywhere else to lay your sorry head!"

I watched the red paper fall into the trashcan. Catching Father's gaze, I quickly fixed my eyes on my book and turned the page.

"You missing the point Herb, you missing the whole goddamn point! You know I appreciate this, man, but all I am trying to say is that we all need to go down there and stand beside a brother trying to help our people. You got it good here. Got a bedroom, sitting room, and a kitchen, but all some folks got is one lil' old raggedy room for them and their three or four kids; no electricity half the time; rotten floorboards. And if they have running water, it's might near as dark as me. Judy, you remember Judy don't you? Couple of weeks back, Judy told me she nodded off and when she came around a big-assed rat was on her table drinking her baby's milk bottle. And the other day five apartments burnt out of the building around the corner there and killed a whole family. Baby and all. What that baby do to deserve that? Nothing! What they gonna do to make it right? Nothing! They not even gonna try. White folks are gonna keep doing what we keep letting them do!"

I wanted to say that I had seen the rats too when I went over to Cindy's, but I didn't want Father to notice that I was still in the room.

"And just what do you think King gonna do, huh?" Father stressed each word. "He come riding through here like he's some sort of colored knight in shining armor and all of you go running down there to do whatever he tells you to do! A man can not take care of his family from some jail cell! He ain't nothing but an uppity nigger making trouble for the rest of us who are trying to make a decent living."

"That's low brother, that's real low. And your living ain't all that decent to tell the truth! Just say you are too chicken-shit to do what's right, but don't go puttin' down folks who aren't. This may be good enough for you and yours, but I want something better for mine,"

Uncle Byrd squeezed every heated word from between his teeth.

"Byrd, don't you call me out of my name." Father rushed across the room towards Uncle Byrd, stopping less than a foot from him.

"So what you gonna do Herb? Somebody tell you the truth and you can't take that shit can you?"

"You just brain-washed like all them other stupid niggers."

"No your uncle tom ass won't say nothing about damn brain-washed," Uncle Byrd stepped closer to Father.

Father clinched his teeth and hissed, "You are not going to disrespect me in my own house - ," Uncle Byrd was gone before Father finished his sentence.

<u>Damned devil.</u>

"See, this is it. The paper inviting everybody to come out."

"Where you get this from?"

"Father threw it in the trash and I got it out when I was emptying the cans this morning." Cyndi and I sat crouched, knees to chest, underneath the window outside of my apartment. Looking at the crumpled red paper, a little greasy and slightly torn, we read. I knew some of the words already, others I had memorized from the night before.

"July 10, 1966. When was that? What's today?" Cyndi rolled her eyes upward and creased her eyebrows. She held both hands up and using her fingers started counting the days.

"It was Sunday."

"Yeah, that's what I thought." Cyndi wrapped her arms around her knees. I knew that she hadn't really figured it out.

"Sol..solly..solly-der," Cyndi tried to sound it out.

"Soldier Field." I said, a little irritated.

"Uhmph." She nodded a grown-up nod as if she was letting me know that I had pronounced it correctly.

"You think Rev. King wrote this?"

"He don't have time to write stuff like this. Probably was one of his helpers. He told him to, though." I raised my eyebrows and looked at Cyndi for a couple of seconds, waiting to see if she had another question. Now, I was the expert and I sat taller than Cyndi for once.

"Why you say 'him'? It could've been a her. What you gonna do with it?"

"I don't know. Keep it, I guess."

When Uncle Byrd left last night, Mama said she would like to go to the rally. One Sunday of missing church wasn't going to hurt. Mr. King is a preacher, and God would be there too. Sunday morning, Mama put on her long-sleeved green and white polka-dot cotton dress to cover the purple blotches on her arms. Father never hit her in the face near Sunday. She sweated all the way to church.

"Ruthie, can't you hear? I said, do you think any white folks went?"

"How would I know Cyndi? Uncle Byrd said there'd be a lot of people there. He say our bodies not slaves anymore, but our minds are."

The way Uncle Byrd said it, I knew he was right. After supper, when I was studying, I took the red paper from my shoe and put it inside my Bible.

"Ruthie, walk down to the market with me, my mama wants some cigarettes." Cyndi had it bad about telling you to do stuff, instead of asking. Mama said she was too grown, and that I should make new friends. I simply nodded, knowing that no one else wanted to be my friend.

The block was noisy again, even though it was still extra hot outside. Today it was a different type of noisy. Instead of the loud yelling back and forth, music blasting, and dominoes slamming, there was a loud murmur. Like everybody was telling the same secret loud enough for everybody else to overhear.

"What do you want?" The old leathery white face didn't give us time to make it up to the counter, before giving us rough talk.

"Three cigarettes please" Cyndi said, holding up three fingers to show that she knew how to count and couldn't be cheated.

The old white leathery face looked over our heads and continued his conversation with the young man putting the cans of peas on the shelf.

"I knew there would be problems. That meeting got 'em all stirred up. They shouldn't have let nothing like that happen in the first place. I don't know why Daly don't just run him back down there to wherever he came from. We didn't have a problem until him and his goons came up here making trouble." The white leathery face looked down at his newspaper and then turned to look for the cigarettes on the shelves behind the counter. "Somebody ought to have just dropped a bomb smack dab in the middle of that stadium. That would've got rid of our problem right there."

"It wasn't the rally that made them angry," the man stopped putting the cans on the shelf. He had an accent and dark olive-colored skin. He wasn't Spanish or Puerto Rican, he was a foreigner. "I heard that it started because the commissioner sent police to shut off their fire hydrants. They shut off one near Roosevelt, I believe, and say a negro boy turned it on again. You cannot blame him. We used ours too. It has been a really hot summer." His accent was thick. He wiped the sweat from his face with the green apron that was tied around his neck and at his waist.

"If you'd come off from the west side, over there with all them gringos, you wouldn't be so hot. Seems to me like you got some sort of fixation or something." The white, leathery face turned back around towards the counter with three cigarettes in his hand. He stared at the olive man who broke the gaze by returning to his work stocking the shelves. Now, he was neatly arranging cans of carrots. "Say they been running through the streets, breaking up stuff, looting, all sorts of carrying on for almost three days now. Like they're crazy. Well, most of 'em are. It's their nature, I guess. A lot more trouble than they're worth."

He put the three cigarettes down on the counter and Cyndi did the same with her money, making sure he realized that she had done so. She slapped her money onto the counter like a domino. I almost expected her to call, "Twenty-five and that's no jive!" The white, leathery face still hadn't looked at us. He looked over our heads, looked for the cigarettes, talked over our heads, and looked down at the money. He counted the money twice twice and then told us to get on out of the store. I wasn't really sure he knew that we were real until he told us to get out.

"You should have seen it Herb, the look on his face when that TV came busting through the window at him. If it wasn't for that TV, I'd probably be layed out somewhere down on Roosevelt right now. You get used to seeing TV's go into pawnshops, it's a whole 'nother thing when they're coming out! I tell you, he had me by the arm..." Uncle Byrd stood with his feet apart and arms behind his back replaying the scene. "...and then all of a sudden, wham! Right there at his feet." Uncle Byrd jumped and looked down at the floor like the tv was really right there in our livingroom. I almost giggled. "Barely missed him. Damn pig, should've got him in the head, like he got me in mine with that damned billy club."

"Byrd, come over here to the table, so I can take a look at your head. There's better light over here, come on and sit down." Mama pulled the chair out from the kitchen table. Uncle Byrd couldn't stop talking while Mama was tending the gash on his forehead. He sat slumped down in the chair with his head tilted over the back. I took my time at the sink, quietly drying and putting away the dishes that mama had washed.

"He let my arm go and I took off quicker than a bullet. I know his face was red then." Uncle Byrd laughed.

"None of you had any business down there anyway. You are lucky it was just your head," Father paced back and forth in front of Uncle Byrd.

"Man, we got to do something. We can't just sit around here waiting for, Ow! Bea, what you doin?"

"Sit still Byrd, I'm just cleaning this, you don't want an infection setting up." Mama's voice was timidly sweet. "You're as bad as Ruthie with your whining." She glanced up at Father as if she were making sure she still had his permission to help Uncle Byrd. Then, she pretended that she didn't enjoy being so close to him, like it was a chore to help him, not a desire.

"What you cleaning it with, gasoline? Turpentine? I thought you liked me, Bea." Uncle Byrd could always make Mama smile. On the rare occasions that you saw her teeth, Uncle Byrd was usually around. She became human in his presence.

"I tell you Herb, man, you should've been there. It would've been like that time we went poking at that bull in the prairie by big mama's house. That bull came after us, shoot we barely made it over that fence in time. Remember that?" Uncle Byrd's laugh was contagious and Mama giggled aloud, but quickly stiffened again.

"It was a pasture, not a prairie," Father's eyes softened up for a brief moment, and then went hard again.

"You just won't be satisfied until you dead or in jail somewhere." Father sat down at the kitchen table. "So where was your fearless leader? He started all of this, but I bet he wasn't down there getting his head banged in. Leave that to the fools."

"Aw Herb don't start in on that again. Besides, Reverend King didn't have anything to do with this. Black folks are just sick-and-tired is all. What the hell is the harm with cooling off in the hydrant? Everybody everywhere does it. But no, they want to come into our neighborhood messing with us. I bet they didn't turn off nobody else's hydrant. I wish I could've seen that little girl throw that bucket of water on that pig." Uncle Byrd laughed. I smiled, pretending that I was the little girl and Uncle Byrd was excited because of me. He didn't say my name because he didn't want to get me into trouble. The glass that I was drying became my bucket and I was standing beside the fire hydrant.

"So, I guess that's what you new negroes do with your time; just go rioting and stealing and tearing up your own neighborhood. That makes a lot of sense. Bea his head is as good as it's gonna get. Make me some coffee." Mama patted Uncle Byrd on the shoulder and went over to the stove. Its deep mustard color matched the cushions in the kitchen chairs. I handed her a pot to boil the water before she even asked.

"Anyway, I bet old Daly will start paying some attention now." Uncle Byrd got up from the table, went into the living room, inched the heavy maroon and gold curtain away from the window, peeped out, and quickly dropped the curtain to cover the window again.

"Uhmph," Father shook his head from side-to-side and then it was quiet.

CHAPTER

5

The announcement came with a stern face and steel eyes right after Father's prayer over our dinner. It was the same prayer that me, mama, God, and anyone else who has ever eaten with us has already heard. Reaching over the fish, the fried potatoes, and the sliced tomatoes to the plate of white bread, Father casually announced that we would be moving to Texas. There was no sense of questioning or concern. The decision had been made, and the announcement was not so much a courtesy as a directive. His chest puffed up and he took a bite of the bread. Mama and I waited in silence for further explanation or just conversation on the matter, but he ate like there was none needed. He was wearing his I Am Man face.

Uncle Byrd busted through the front door like something or someone was chasing after him. He dropped his bag, and rushed to the empty seat at the table. Without stopping to wash his face or hands, he grabbed for the plate of fried fish.

"How's my family doing this evening?"

"Herbert has exciting news," Mama said, but I couldn't tell is she was talking to Uncle Byrd or to the fish on her plate. I looked over at Uncle Byrd, waiting for him to ask questions. Father glared over at mama, who in turn, never lifted her head. She refused to see the warning of what would happen to her later, when they were alone.

"Really! What's up Herb?"

"I have accepted the invitation from True Mount to take over as their pastor. We will be moving to Texas," Father voice was strengthened with pride. He held his fork in his right hand as his left elbow supported him and the weight of his announcement. Bad manners. His rolled sleeve stopped right before his elbow, revealing his forearm resting on the table beside his plate.

"You what? Man, what's going on in your head? You trying to be a real preacher now?"

"Watch yourself, Byrd."

"Where at in Texas?"

"Billings, Texas. Not far from where Big Mama used to stay."

"You done lost your mind. What would you go to Texas for, especially down there? You know your neighbors gonna be a cow and a chicken. Besides, what are you gonna do for money? You been at the packing plant for over seven years now, you just gonna leave that?"

"First of all, my money is not your business, and anyway I've been cut back to three days a week at the plant for over three months now."

"But what are you going to do in Texas, raise chickens or something?"

"The church has made a very generous offer. They've got a house already furnished and a car waiting for me. Plus, I will be getting a monthly stipend. . . and any special offerings, of course."

"Man, you done lucked-up on your biggest hustle so far. Maybe, I'll start preaching. And God said, uh, be kind, uh, to your neighbors, uh, and pass the collection plate, uh." Uncle Byrd slapped the table hard with his last 'uh'. He leaned back in his chair and laughed so hard he almost tipped over.

"Shut your wretched mouth, Byrd! Don't go playing with the Lord."

Byrd looked at Father or he looked through Father. "Man, whatever. So when all this supposed to happen?"

"We'll be leaving in January."

"That's right around the corner. Well, Miss Bea, you ready for country life?"

"Yeah, she ready," Father answered before Mama could clear the food from her mouth.

When the blur from my tears had cleared, I looked over at Mama and realized that she too was probably blinded by the water in her eyes.

"What's wrong baby girl? Bea?" Uncle Byrd looked at each face around the table. "Herb don't tell me this is your first time telling them about this?"

"Byrd, shut your stupid mouth, everyone is fine." Father clinched his fist and teeth and looked at Mama, who in turn flinched and covered the once mahogany now blue bruise on her arm. "Anyway, this is my family and I am responsible for the decision making. I know what's best. Beatrice and Ruthie both will be fine with any decision I make."

Uncle Byrd stared at mama's hand still covering her bruise.

"You mean, you're fine. Whatcha' gonna do with your stuff here?"

"Probably sell it. We don't need to take much with us. We'll be going by bus, so we'll travel as light as possible."

Somehow I knew 'travel as light as possible' did not include getting rid of any of his things. Uncle Byrd fell silent for a while. I could tell that he was reviewing his own thoughts by the way he looked upward as he chewed his food. I accidentally let a tear slip from my eye to my cheek.

"The dinner table is no place for all of that," Father said. "Now straighten your face, before I give you something to cry about. No need in making yourself more ugly."

My eyes were stinging and before I was able to stop the flow, tears were streaming down my face.

"It's okay Ruthie," the shaky sweetness in Mama's voice was too much. It was so sweet that it made me sick to my stomach. She lifted my chin and looked into my wet eyes. "Go and wipe your face." How could she tell me that it was okay? How could she sit there and lie to me? Why did she look into my eyes, when she wouldn't even lift her own eyes from the fish a few minutes ago? I hated everything about this moment. I hated that we were moving. I hated that I was crying. I hated that she was so weak. But most of all, I hated him.

"You sit right there!" Between saying those words and slapping Mama's face, Father stood up toppling over his chair. "Beatrice, don't you ever contradict what I tell that girl! Ruthie, I said straighten your face up and that is what I mean!"

Uncle Byrd stood up. Both of his fists were balled-up and every muscle in his face was tight.

"You're a sorry son-of-a-bitch! You feel your balls now? Hitting on women, terrorizing kids, that make you feel your balls? You always talking about a damned devil. You ought to know him well. He always looking back at you every time you look in a mirror, Mr. Preacher man." He bumped Father's shoulder as he passed him, picked up his bag, and was out the front door before Mama could move her hand away from the reddish print that was now on the left side of her face.

Father breathed heavily above the silence. Mama gave me a sickening smile, put her napkin in her lap with the hand that had covered her cheek, and picked up her fork with the other.

More ugly. He had said, "More ugly." I look like him, not her.

CHAPTER

6

I did not want my bangs to turn back into the drawn-up, sponge puff that they had been before mama pressed them. That is why I hoped that she would slow down. I didn't want to sweat.

We usually walk to church together on Sunday mornings, but Father had already left. It was just mama and me walking the two blocks down and one over to New Hebron Baptist Church. It was still early, but the sun was beaming down on my forehead threatening to ruin my fresh press.

"Ruthie, keep up." Mama yelled, but didn't look back. She just kept on walking, her long-legged strides were like three steps to my one. I held my bangs down with one hand, and cuffed my Bible with the other. I pretended that it was my purse, black patent leather like the one Ms. Dora had given me for my last birthday. Father said that I was too young to carry it, so mama put it in the top of the closet in the bedroom. Every now and again, I stack a telephone book in one of the kitchen chairs so that I can climb up and look at it.

I let out a deep sigh when we finally made it to the steps of the church. Just before we walked through the doors, Mama pulled her handkerchief from her handbag. She placed her gloved hand beneath my chin and lifted my face up towards hers.

"Let me wipe some of this shine off of your face," she said as if the thought exasperated her.

Cool air welcomed us into the sanctuary. I always pretended that the church was my home. I always felt rich there. It was the most beautiful place that I had ever been. The pews were padded and covered with burgundy fabric that matched the fabric draped across the wall behind the pulpit. Two gold candelabras stood on the floor in front of the pulpit, one on each side, and on some Sundays, seven candles glowed from each of them. Five beautiful mahogany wood chairs graced the pulpit; the biggest one, the centerpiece, was for Reverend Johansen. Sunlight shined through the stain-glassed windows making tiny rainbows throughout the church. Once, a rainbow was in my lap during the entire morning service.

Some of the people in the congregation turned and looked as mama and I entered the sanctuary; we were late.

"And the father, when he saw that his prodigal son was coming home…" Reverend Johansen was already preaching. "…he prepared a feast. You see it doesn't matter where you've been, all you have to do is come back home. Come up out of the pig's pen. Come up out of your backslidden ways. Come up out of adultery and fornication. Come up out of your lying and your cheating." He stood neatly tucked behind the podium wrapped in his robe that matched the color of the pews and the fabric on the walls behind the pulpit. He slapped the podium with the palm of his hand each time he said the word "come." Father was in the pulpit, to the left of where Reverend Johansen stood preaching. His arms folded and legs crossed, he slightly nodded occasionally.

Just this morning, I had shined his Stacy Adams while mama pressed his shirt.

"Repent! And turn from your wicked ways." Reverend Johansen turned and looked into the choir stand, and then into the pulpit, and then back again at the congregation. I couldn't imagine that there were actually any sinners there, but I looked for them as he looked. Everyone that I could see, sat upright, knees pressed together or crossed, with serious looks on their faces.

"Sit back." Mama said through clenched teeth as she pinched my leg. There was hardly any movement as everyone listened to the sermon. Once, a woman, who was a visitor, had stood and clapped during the sermon. The usher came up from behind, tapped her on the shoulder, and whispered something into her ear. The lady sat down for only a minute before she picked up her purse and her Bible and left the church.

"Because I am here to tell you," Reverend Johansen spoke quietly, solemnly. "Neither liars nor adulterers, fornicators nor thieves, will see the kingdom."

Although I had only been there a short time, I was glad that it was almost over. I couldn't wait to see the dresses, and shoes, and gloves, and jewelry, and hats that everyone was wearing. Sunday was always a parade of the very finest clothes and jewelry. In the winter, some people even wore fur coats. I would wear my fur coat too when I married my rich doctor. It would be floor-length with a hat to match. I would wear my diamond rings over my silk gloves, and carry my Bible in a leather case with my name engraved on a golden plate, Mrs. Rich Doctor.

After church let out and Mama had spoken to the few women who spoke to her, she and I walked home together and alone. Father was walking Sister Jesse home because she wasn't feeling well. Mama was quiet all the way home. No "keep up," or "stop dragging!" It was a lonely walk home.

CHAPTER

7

The muscles in my legs burned as I ran. It was so dark that I could hardly see anything in front of me. Gasping for breath, I ran along a tiny trail through a forest. The only things moving were me and the thing that was chasing me. Large trees hung overhead and the dark limbs and vines slapped my face, arms, and bare legs as I struggled to get away. I glanced back and saw a two-headed beast with large red eyes still coming after me. It had scales and huge spikes lined his back from the top of his head to the end of his lizard-like tail. Showing his huge sharp teeth, he roared and sent forth his forked tongue to capture me. My heart leapt and I tried to run faster, but fell instead. I rolled over onto my back and there he was, standing over me. He dipped his head to devour me. Just as I braced myself for the pain, he let out a huge howl and fell to the ground.

Then, I saw someone standing behind the dragon. With both hands holding a shiny silver sword, her arms were still raised above her head. I tried to get up, so that I could run again, but was paralyzed. This lady frightened me as much as the dragon had. She walked over to me, never lowering the sword. I looked up and realized that the someone was simply a girl, and a small one at that. Surprised, I realized that the girl was me. I scrambled to my feet and stood face-to-face with myself in the dark shadows. We would have been identical were it not for her eyes. Her eyes were those of a savage beast, they were wild and unfeeling. She gave me a broad smile and I realized that her sword shined brightly like it was brand new, but her teeth were covered with blood.

I sat straight up in my bed, panting like I was still running from the dragon of my dream. The room was dark and everything was quiet except for the box fan at the doorway of the room. Its low moan and rotating blades blew the sheet that mama used as a divider to separate my side of the room from her and Father's side.

When I finally caught my breath, I looked around to assure myself of where I was and that I was safe. My mouth was dry and a glass of water seemed like a good idea. I swung my legs over the edge of the bed, readying myself to make a trip to the kitchen, but there was no moon or streetlight to show me the way. I could hear the whistle that Father's nose made as he slept. It wasn't really a snore just a whistle sort of like a teakettle. When I thought about possibly bumping into things and making enough noise to awaken him, my heart raced again. I decided against getting a drink. The morning should come soon enough.

Finally, after I had calmed myself once again, I lay back down. Twice over, I said the Lord's Prayer in my mind, hoping that God would somehow hear and let me sleep dreamlessly for the rest of the night.

Winter came all of a sudden and caught most people by surprise. Up until the beginning of January, Cyndi and I walked to school wearing only light sweaters or jackets to block the wind. Today, however, I met her in front of her building and we both laughed at the sight of the other in her puffy coat, hat, scarf, and gloves.

"Okay, meet you at lunch," Cyndi turned to me as we headed towards the fifth grade classroom. She had been left back last year, and now, I dreaded each day of going to my sixth grade class alone. Before, she had protected me from many of the attacks of our classmates.

"Okay, see you later."

When the tardy bell rang, I was safely seated in my chair in front of Mrs. Kowalski. She seemed genuinely saddened when she read mama's note saying that I was leaving for Texas. She offered that I was one of the brightest colored students that she had ever taught. We took those placement tests at the beginning of the school year, and I scored highest in the entire school. A white boy scored second highest and they skipped him up to sixth grade. He said he was Italian and Jewish. I said he was white. Either way, he was now in the sixth grade. With only one week left, Mrs. Kowalski smiled at me more often than she had before and even called on me to be her helper.

I was happy when she asked me to pass out the readers, but my heart pounded at the thought of walking up and down the aisles for everyone to see.

Mrs. Kowalski gave me the stack of books and starting at the first row from the door, I passed by each of my classmates allowing them to choose their own book from the stack. When I got to the second seat of the fourth row, my hands grew shaky. I looked up from the stack of books and noticed Carl Brown giggling at something he had just finished telling the boy behind him. In the first grade, Carl had used the big gap in his front teeth to spit apple juice on me and I had been his target ever since. The chestnut brown skin and red hair made Carl look a bit peculiar to me, but it didn't seem to stop him from being popular with all the other kids. Now two desks away from him, my legs seemed as if they were made of creamed butter.

To my surprise, Carl chose his reader and put it on his desk. Relieved and more steady, I turned to walk away. I felt his hand in the middle of my back between my shoulder blades. With his swift push, my neck jerked as I lost my balance and went tumbling down. I fell hard, but not before banging my elbow on the corner of a desk. The remaining readers sprawled on the floor in front of me.

"Carl Brown! You go to the office this moment!" Mrs. Kowalski leaped up from her chair and came over to help me to my feet. As I dusted myself off, I realized that all of the other kids were laughing. He had planned it, probably from the first moment Mrs. Kowalski asked me to pass out the readers. My eyes were stinging, but I would not cry.

Lunch had not come soon enough. I walked into the lunchroom looking around for Cyndi. She wasn't there yet, so I sat at the table where we always ate and waited for her to come. I had just put my brown paper bag, worn from use the day before, on the table in front of me, when Carl came over with a couple of other boys.

"How you like your trip?" Carl laughed at his own joke and then the other boys joined him.

"Leave her alone, Carl," Cyndi came and sat across from me.

"Who you think you are, her guardian angel or something?"

I had decided in second grade that the best thing to do was just to ignore him. When I opened my bag the smell of fried fish rushed out to meet me. Mama had packed me a sandwich using last night's leftovers. I unwrapped the wax paper and put the sandwich in front of me. Carl licked the palm of his hand and then smashed it down on top of my sandwich.

Before I could think of anything to say, I had already jumped out of my chair and hit Carl in the jaw. The surprise of the blow knocked him to the floor. I hopped on top of him and punched over and over again. When I got tired of punching, I clawed at his face with my fingernails. I was trying to get his eyes, but he kept turning his face away.

Someone pulled us apart and first we went to see the principal and then the nurse. In the nurse's office, I prayed for God to forgive Carl's meanness and dug some of his skin from beneath my fingernails.

Back in class, Carl mentioned that he was going to kill me. He couldn't break my silence though. I figured that if he was going to kill me, he would have to do it soon, since I only had a few days before I left for Texas.

Then before Art, Mrs. Kowalski announced that a snowstorm was coming and that we were being sent home early.

"Go straight home." She looked at Carl and then at some of the other boys, but mostly at Carl.

All the way home, Cyndi talked about how I had really put it on Carl. I wasn't happy about the whole fight, but I wasn't sad. Nevertheless, no matter what Cyndi said, she couldn't break my silence either.

The snow fell harder than ever, shutting down the whole city, and to my relief, that included schools. With only two days until we were scheduled to leave, the snow probably upset Carl just as much as it did Father who got more irritated the longer he stayed inside with me and mama.

We had sold most of our things to neighbors and church friends before the storm had hit. The only things left in our apartment were the things that we were taking, couldn't sell, or that Uncle Byrd would use. The navy blue arm chair with the ripped seat cushion was still there. We still had one of the end tables because the man who had bought the matching coffee table could only afford one of the end tables. Father wouldn't go down on the price, so it was still there.

Sitting in the only chair left in the living room, I looked out the window and watched Father struggle to hold the collar of his huge brown coat over his ears. He had decided to fight the storm to get to the corner market and use the pay phone. He said he needed to call deacon something-or-other and let him know that we were snowed in and may not be arriving as planned.

The brightness of the snow shot a pain through my eyes, but I looked anyway. The satisfaction of not being able to leave Chicago and seeing Father lose his balance in the snow warmed my whole body. It broke my silence.

"Can I have some milk, mama?"

Walking around the nearly empty apartment reminded me that I would be leaving as soon as the snow stopped falling so heavily. I was going to a place that I knew nothing about. The only way to get out of this mess was to make believe, and so I did.

When Father went out, I pretended that he wasn't going to come back and that mama and I would have to stay here. Uncle Byrd would stay with us. Sometimes I believed it and I felt relief, but Father kept coming back.

The knock at the door surprised me, but not as much as the person who stood there when mom answered. It was the white face. With folded arms, he peeped from beneath his hat.

"Is this the preacher's house? I thought I may be able to get a little help from you people." He said that he had just come down to check on the store, and on the way out his car had stalled. "I hate to bother you, but that old phone at the store isn't much good. It's been out for going on a month now, and I can't seem to get anyone out to fix it. I was wondering if I could make a call."

Mom looked confused. Father had gone to use the pay phone at the store at least five times since the storm hit.

"I'm sorry mister, but we don't have a phone." Mom apologized for being poor. "Would you like to come in and warm up?"

The white face looked at mama like he was seriously considering her offer, but without a word he turned and walked back into the snowstorm.

Father came home shortly after the white face had left. AS soon as he walked through the door, I started to tell him that the white face had come to our house, but mom told me to shut up and sent me to the bedroom.

The grown-ups acted strange when it was time to go. They acted as if nothing was changing. They acted happy. Cyndi and I didn't play along with them. We didn't smile when we said goodbye. We didn't stop our tears. And we didn't lie about seeing each other soon. We hung on for dear life when we hugged.

"She can come visit you next summer." Ms. Hawkins pried Cyndi away from me.

"You are big girls, you shouldn't be carrying on this way," Mama said pulling me to her side. She must've forgotten that I'd seen her crying in Ms. Dora's arms. Both Mama and Ms. Hawkins' voices trembled behind their smiles. Watching Cyndi and I, they looked like they were watching a three-legged dog struggle down a crowded street on a hot summer day or a maimed kitten.

I just kept playing Ms. Hawkins' words over-and-over in my head.

On the bus, Mama kept her face towards the window. Her warm breath made a steam circle, the kind that I would draw pictures or write my name in if it were mine. I think she was trying to hide the bold tears that were racing from her eyes to her chin. She had tried to call her daddy when we were at the bus depot. We had left Father reading his paper and stood in line to use the payphone. When it was finally her turn, mama dropped her coin in the slot.

"Good morning," she said gently. "May I speak with Henry Durham please?" Mama twisted the telephone cord around her finger and waited. Her eyes widened, "Hi Daddy, it's me, Beatrice." Her faint smile faded as she pulled the receiver away from her ear and stared at it.

She dropped in another coin and pushed the buttons quickly. She smoothed out her dress, "Good morning," this time her voice was trembling. "May I please speak with Henry

Durham once more?" She twisted the cord. Quickly she said, "Daddy, I'm leaving, I just"

She dropped her head and pulled the receiver to her chest.

"Come on sister. We're waiting here you know," the man in line behind mama huffed.

"Yes, just a second. Please." And she dropped another coin into the slot. "Henry Durham, please," mama breathed deeply. "But, I know he's there. Well, why? No, thank you." Mama slammed the receiver onto its hook. She grabbed my arm and we walked back over to where Father was sitting.

I had met my grandfather once before when I was four. It wasn't a Sunday, but mama had made me wear a dress, tights, and my church shoes. It was exciting being so close to a factory with puffs of smoke filling the air above it. I hopped and skipped around.

"Be still," Mama kept saying, "you're going to mess your hair up." But she wasn't really looking at me, so I kept hopping and skipping.

We were at the gate. He was so big, much bigger than Father. He was dirty like a factory worker, but he didn't hang his head like them. He didn't smile. The black smudge on his forehead held my attention, keeping me in one place the whole time he and mama talked. It matched the stuff on his hands and clothes. I watched it grow shorter as he wrinkled his forehead.

"I can't have no grandchild, because my daughter already dead," the smudge was long and was very still.

But I was right there. I wanted to shout, "Here I am," but thought better. He was so tall that he didn't even see me. I had wanted him to pick me up and give me something from one of his pockets like a quarter or candy even though he was dirty. But after he had said this, he went back into the factory.

Mama said my grandpa really loved me and she cried all the way home after I asked why he didn't love her too. When she told Ms. Dora about our meeting, Ms. Dora told her to let it go. "You chose Herbert. Now you got to live with your decision."

The bus was crowded with black people. The smell of fried foods broke through greasy brown paper bags. There was even a man darker than me and Father, but mostly they were just normal black people. I thought about

Ms. Dora. I had heard her tell mama how black folks were escaping the south any way they could. I remembered thinking that me, Father, and mama would be the only blacks on the bus to Texas.

"Mama, what happened to that white lady who bought her ticket ahead of us?"

With a quick flicker of her hand, Mama waved my question away without ever turning her face away from the window.

The man who was darker than me and Father was seated in the aisle seat across from me and mama. Though the bus was crowded, the seat next to him stayed empty. Everyone quickly opted for a different seat, even when he offered to scoot over for them. Overhearing my question, he'd laughed a strong laugh, flashing his much too yellow teeth.

"Sweet, no whitey wan ride wit a bus full of we. Us color may rub off on 'em." He laughed again and gave me a wink like we were bonded by a secret no one else would ever know. I wanted to break the bond, but I knew the struggle would kill me long before the bond would even begin to weaken. We were different and would never be like the other black people on the bus. We can hope, dream, and even pretend, but inside I knew and he must've known too.

Father turned from his seat in front of us and told mama to keep me quiet. She pinched my leg muntil my face was heated with pain and anger. But this did not warm the frigid air that came with his order. I think Father knows too.

"May I have my sweater please?" I mumbled to my black patent leather shoes, hoping that mama would hear.

10

Long stretches of giant trees and twisted roads were in front of and behind us. A low buzz hung in the air for most of the ride. It was the buzz of private talk in a public place.

The man and lady, Jim and Cora, in the row behind us, were planning to be married. They were on their way to tell Cora's parents the good news, and maybe about the baby.

The man in the seat across from father had had his fill of city life. Too much hustle and bustle he said. "Da simple life of the souf is all I need. That's fo sho. No mo city fo me. Dem city women sho are some of the prettiest things I ever done seen. Dey fast spreaders, but dem some fast talkers too. Ain't got nothin' lef but da other half of my pride. My sweet

MaryAnn, she'll take me back tho' and fix my soul. Yeah, my MaryAnn."

The little girl two rows behind us let her voice sail over the buzz. She was proud that she could read the two books that her mother had bought for her at the five-and-dime. She proudly pronounced the single and sometimes compound words. Except for the slow pace and a few muddled words, she read pretty well. The girl, with her two braids pulling her eyes back into a slant, tried to read every passing sign. "Sara Jane walked to the market. Inside she saw milk, eggs, and cheese." If she got it right, she let out a huge giggle, followed by a, "That's real good," from her mother.

"We're here," the bus driver announced, as we pulled into the lot of a wooden store that looked like something from a storybook. In the middle of nowhere. No shops, no buildings, no factory, no apartments. How could we be here when there was no here? Mama's face was blank, so I couldn't tell if the driver was playing or not.

Tin covered the bottom half of the store and the top was painted a dark green. Hinckley's Store, according to the hand painted sign, was also the bus depot. Red clay dirt and rocks covered by leftover, icy slush was the parking lot. A tin carport attached to the front of the store was the depot's waiting area. Long, clear icicles, not like the flimsy silver ones on our Christmas tree, hung from the carport. Chopped wood was stacked along the edges of the depot.

At first, the frosty window perfectly framed the pink faces of a man and woman. Once the bus doors opened and we began to shuffle off, the faces disappeared and the window shade was let down. It was a ghost town and the pink faces were ghosts. They only show up when they think you're not looking.

Ghosts won't let go of the past. They try to hold onto things that don't belong to them anymore. That's why they haunt houses. If you try to move in, they try to scare you away. They don't want things to change. Don't want you to have what they believe is theirs. Don't want you to stumble up on their secrets hidden in secret places. But ghosts don't need heat, and there was smoke coming from the chimney.

I pressed my eyes together and prayed quickly. "God, please protect us from any ghosts and stuff. Amen."

The sun beamed, but it didn't stop the cold and the wind from whipping through thin coats, making eyes water and noses run. Poofs of smoke burst from the mouths of anyone who spoke or laughed or let out an open-mouthed breath. A sharp wind carried the scent of housecleaning on Saturday morning mixed with smoke. Father stood tall. Shielding his eyes with his right hand, he looked around breathing in his new power. The little girl from two rows back pointed to the store's sign and mispronounced Hinckley's. Her mother with her pinned bun at the back of her head, small eyeglasses, suit and matching gloves, helped her sound it out.

Not put off by her mistake, the little girl moved on to the next sign, "Fresh smoked bacon." Her mother smiled, "That's real good."

Father smoothed his jacket and stood straight. The pride in his pose was as striking as the giant trees towering over us. The little girl giggled with excitement as she read the sign above the store's door, "No Colored Allowed!" She mispronounced 'allowed', but it didn't matter.

A police car drove past the bus depot, turned around and drove past again. It did this three times and then the bus pulled away. That's when I could see the people standing across the highway. Black. Behind them, a long mint green car cast bright sunlight into my squinting eyes. The older man pushed his hat back off of his forehead, and used his hand to shade the sun from his eyes while he looked over the people at the bus depot. With quick bow-legged strides, he headed across the highway, fixing his hat along the way. The other two, a woman and a man, both younger, struggled to keep up with him.

The younger man fought to keep his coat closed. If it had been red, he would have looked like Superman crossing the highway.

"Revun' Johnson, dat you?" the old man's wide smile showed his big stained teeth. He sang his words like Ms. Dora. Taking off his brown felt hat with one hand, he reached the other towards Father.

"Yes, I am Reverend Johnson," Father pronounced each word like when he talks to white people. The old man grabbed Father's hand and shook it hard, almost like he was mad, but his wide smile said differently.

I took my gloved hands from my coat pockets just in case someone wanted to shake my hand. I could curtsy too. I saw a little white girl do it on tv. Mama had said that it was proper. Father would be proud. My heart started beating real fast, but I stood still.

"Yessuh, I 'spected that was you. I saw you from cross the way there and says to Jessie May and Tommy, that there's our pastor."

"Sho' did. Uhm huh," the other two chimed in.

"These here your bags? Come on, let us get you out of this cold." The old man put his hat back on, covering his tight steel gray hair.

His eyes grabbed me and when I tried to look away, I couldn't. They were blue. But he was black. Not the blue of an ink pen, but a pale blue that could almost be gray. He grabbed two of our bags, and at the nod of his head the man and woman scrambled to pick up the others.

"This here is Jessie May Carter, she the Sunday School secretary and that there's Tommy Henson. He one of your deacons, but we can tend to formal 'ductions once we get you out of this here cold." Crossing the highway, even Father had trouble keeping up with the old man. Mama didn't try.

The car smelled like peppermint. It was already a little warm, so I only had a slight chill from being outside. Deacon Henson drove, and Father sat up front. The old man wouldn't let it be any other way. I sank deep into the leather seat between Father and Deacon Henson. Mama sat in the back between the old man and Sister Carter.

"Dese bones ain't too old fo me to climb into that back seat. No sir. Not to dis'spect my pastor and put 'im in the bucket seat. Ain't that old yet," the old man laughed. I laughed too because he sounded funny. Father's eyes cut me off, but the old man kept on. I liked him, so I kept on laughing, just not on the outside though.

I tried to peek into the rearview mirror to see his eyes again, but I couldn't see him.

"Well suh, I ain't told you who I was have I," the old man followed this with a hefty laugh. "I'm Deacon Julius Hall. I reckon they consider me the head deacon. I jus' tries to keep everything in line is all. You sho' have a nice family here. We just pleased to have you all." Deacon Hall's voice rumbled inside my belly as he talked, I could feel his words warming me.

"That there is where Lil' Joe Clayton and his family used to stay before they got burned out. They down near Mt. Tabor now, but they still fellowships with us."

The rest of the ride was full of Deacon Hall's big laughter and 'ductions.' "There yonder is where Mr. Charlie Clemmings lives. He a good white man. Not too many of those 'round here ya know. Over there is some more of our church folks, the Lincolns." Big fields with cows and horses ran along the highway. There were no tall buildings. There were no factories. There were no corner stores with men cursing and drinking. There weren't any street lights to remind kids that it was time to go inside. It was only Deacon Hall's voice that kept me from being lonely.

Two deer stood alongside the road when we went through what Deacon Hall called 'dead man's curve.' It was more like a u-turn.

"Many a accident done happened right here. Ya'll remember that one with James Earl?"

"Lord, lord that sho' was a mess, God bless his soul," in the rear view mirror I could see Sister Carter frown her mouth and shake her head.

"Yep, and there were plenty mo 'fore that. So, Revun' you be careful with this one. I don't know if you got tricky ones like this up north."

Giant trees hovered over the road but didn't block the sunlight. There were none so big in Chicago. No apartment buildings or neighborhoods sat off in the distance. Every once in a while, we would pass a house sitting a little ways away from the highway. Each one looked a lot like the one before it. The small wood-framed houses all seemed to need a fresh coat of paint. Small dirt pathways led into yards that were mostly red dirt and rocks with patches of grass scattered throughout. Empty swings

and chairs sat on crowded porches. The cars
that were parked in these yards looked like the
ones in Chicago that hadn't been moved in
years. I imagined that the insides of the houses
were small and musky, but the darkness made it
hard to believe that real people were living
inside.

Deacon Henson studied the road, never
turning his head to answer any of Deacon Hall's
questions or comments, not that one was
required. Both of his ashy hands were fastened
to the steering wheel. Whiffs of his peppermint
candy floated over my face. Reaching into the
pocket of his button-less coat, he handed me a
peppermint without ever looking away from the
road.

I lowered my head and whispered,
"Thank you," loudly enough for him to know I
said it, but quietly enough for Father not to hear
me.

Deacon Henson pulled off the highway
into the yard of a white house. It was bigger
than the others we had passed. Perfect black
shutters covered each of the windows. Like the
other houses, this house had a porch and a
swing. This one didn't need any paint though.
Concrete steps led up to the screen door that

covered the large white one. A hint of spring surrounded the house, even with the ice stained with red dirt on the ground.

"Well Revun', First Lady, this here's your new home fuh as long as God's willin' you to be here with us. I hope it's to your liking," Deacon Hall proudly announced from the back seat.

Father's face relaxed, but he quickly recovered himself and said, "Fine, Deacon, this looks fine," as if he'd ever lived in such a place before.

I pressed against Father as he was getting out of the car, trying to get into the house as quickly as possible. I darted around him and headed for the porch. He caught my shoulder before I made it to the steps. Looking up at him, I felt the coldness of his 'get yourself together' glance. I wanted to ask if anybody else lived here, but thought better of it.

The smell of pine cleaner and bleach met us when Deacon Hall opened the front door. Except for the bed in the living room, the house was nicely decorated. Father and mama had a bedroom, I had my own bedroom, and there was one to spare. I thought about Cyndi. I couldn't wait to write her and tell her about the perfect white house. I hadn't seen any other children in the yards we'd passed. But it was cold outside; maybe they were inside the dark houses.

Deacon Hall patted my shoulder with his heavy hand and finishing a conversation with my father said, "and there's plenty of chil'ren for lil' Miss. Ruthie to take up company with." I was relieved, but confused, since I hadn't made my concerns known, only thought it. Deacon Hall gave me a wide grin and a wink. It was like I had always known him.

"Deacon, come here, quick!" Sister Carter yelled from the kitchen where she was showing mama the pantry. Mama and Sister Carter were huddled together in the corner. My eyes following their hard stares; my heart made its way to my stomach. One of the first Sunday School lessons I learned was about Adam and Eve and the snake. Now, here it was in the center of the kitchen floor of the perfect house. Only its slight movement and lifted head kept it from being a large black 'S'. Lowering its head, it slithered towards mama and Sister Carter. One of Deacon Hall's hearty laughs broke through the stiff silence.

"That ain't nothin' but a lil' ole' chicken snake. Ya'll all hemmed up in that corner like it was a bear or something. He 'bout more scared of you than you are of him."

Deacon Henson ran into the kitchen and rambled through some of the drawers. With one hand behind his back, he tiptoed over and stooped down behind the snake. Looking up at mama and Sister Carter, he fixed his lips, giving them a silent 'shhhhhh.' The snake inched forward, closer to mama and Sister Carter. Raising a meat cleaver from behind his back, Deacon Henson took off the snake's head in one quick swipe. Mama and Sister Carter ran past the snake into the living room. Father kept his distance behind Deacon Hall, as Deacon Henson picked-up the snake and headed through the living room towards the front door.

With a shaking hand on her heaving chest, Mama whispered a soft and weak thank you.

"Oh, I'm sorry Sister Johnson. I ought to have known better than to laughed at you like that. I'm so sorry. I'll get some more sulfur around this house before sun-down tomorrow," Deacon Hall looked down at the floor instead of at Mama. "I am mighty sorry. I should of known ya'll wasn't used to no snakes or nothing like that being city folks and all. I put sulfur out about a month ago, but I'll be back here and put some more down. I'll make sure you don't have any more run-ins." Deacon Hall held mama's hand like she was a little girl.

"Thank you," she said faintly.

"We gonna go and let you good people get settled in and me and Tommy will bring your car back this evenin' and take you over to the church if you'd like."

"My car," Father stammered.

"There I go again, forgettin' stuff," Deacon Hall chuckled. "That there's your car that we brought you home in. Only we got to go get mine or Tommy's to get us back home once we leave yours here. You reckon you wanna go over to the church this evening?

"Yes, that will be fine."

Father, Mama, and I walked the other three outside. Mama gasped as Father placed his arm around her and pulled her close to his side.

"Smile," I heard him hiss at her from between his teeth, as the three of us stood on the porch waving goodbye.

The house across the road seemed to appear just then. Deacon Hall hadn't pointed it out or made any 'ductions about who stayed there. The house peeked from behind the oversized trees that were scattered throughout the front yard. Bright pink and red roses filled the two huge bushes that stood on each side of the rickety steps leading up to the front door. I couldn't tell if the door was open or closed because of the silvery screen door that reflected the sunlight back into my eyes. The wood of the small house was dark gray, not painted gray, but old, weathered gray. Rusty-orange spots decorated the top of the tin-roof that was much too slanted and much too low. Even I might have to duck down to walk through the house. I could see myself walking, hunched over. A snow-white dog that had been lazying on the porch stood and started to bark in our direction. Magically, a figure appeared. She cracked the screen door to let the dog inside. Then, the house seemed to swallow them both and I could see that the front door was green.

CHAPTER

12

The quietness of the night kept me awake for a long time after mama sent me to bed. I could not tell if I missed the sounds that usually reached above or beneath the sheet that divided our old bedroom to lull me to sleep, or if I simply had too many questions about this new place tumbling over themselves inside my head. My bedroom was right near the front of the house, so I crept back and forth between my bed and the window. The night here was much darker than in Chicago. The space heater in the center of my bedroom didn't seem to warm the floor at all. Each time I slid out of my bed and my feet touched the wood floor, it seemed colder than the time before. I didn't have any slippers. When I unpacked, I'd find a pair of socks to use instead.

I had almost started to dream when the roar of a car and its tires against the rocks in the driveway shook me out of my sleep. A few seconds later another car turned into the driveway. I figured it was Father and the deacons, who had taken him to see the church earlier in the evening. My feet hit the cold floor, and I heard Mama moving around. I didn't run over to the window to try to see the men in case she peeked into my room. I couldn't really tell where she was. I needed to learn a whole new house. People were probably still outside in Chicago. Cold and all, they were probably still sitting on stoops or on cars doing nothing new.

"We'll just come in for a while and wait." It was Deacon Hall.

"What is this all about?" Father's voice was slightly higher than normal.

Mama passed by my bedroom on her way into the living room. "Anything wrong?" she asked.

"Go get us some coffee," Father commanded, as if he hadn't heard her question.

"Well Revun, this ain't the north, things a little different 'round here. They just trying to scare you is all." Deacon Hall was talking a little softer now.

I slid out of bed and tip-toed over to my doorway. I hunched down near the floor instead of sitting, just in case I heard footsteps coming my way and had to spring back over to my bed. I considered the possibility of a snake, like the one from the kitchen, striking upward to bite my butt as I was hunched down on the floor to listen to the grownups talk. But, that thought wasn't enough to send me back to my bed.

"Dey ain't no good Revun." This voice was strange and familiar at the same time. It sounded like Deacon Henson, but angry, which was hard for me to imagine.

"Calm yourself, Tommy! Revun, they knew you was coming in today, and they knew you was from up north. You can just call this the welcome wagon. See. Our last pastor started teachin' bout how they is and ain't supposed to be treating us and what was goin' on in other places."

"That's why they run 'em off!" Deacon Henson wasn't getting any calmer.

"Settle down now Tommy. But you see, that's part of why we asked you here. We figured you being from up north and all, you probably know how to deal with these white folks." Deacon Hall's voice got even softer than before. The old, leathery, white face from the corner store invaded my imagination, and it was hard to shake it from my mind's eye.

"Deacon, I didn't come here to stir up any trouble. I'm here to do God's work." Father clearly pronounced each word.

"Revun, keeping our folks from getting their heads bashed in by white folks is God's work."

Complete silence.

"Here's some coffee to warm you all up. What are you still standing at that door for? Come on in and sit down."

I hopped up, ran, and jumped into my bed when the three honks came from outside. I was so intent on hearing the grown folks talk, that I hadn't even heard this other car pull up. Whoever was outside, was honking and flashing their headlights. I could feel the quickness of my heartbeat. It seemed like it was beating inside my head. I knew to be afraid, but I didn't know why. I lay still until the siren came on, and then, I ran out of my room.

"It's alright Ruthie." I bumped into Mama who had been on her way to get me. I grabbed her waist and she almost had to drag me into the living room. Father and the deacons stopped talking when Mama and I sat down. The sirens blasted again and Deacon Henson leaped up and stomped towards the door.

"Don't give them reason to kill you." Deacon Hall growled at Deacon Henson, who stopped a few feet short of the front door.

The honking, and the flashing, and the sirens went on and on for hours. I cried until my head began to hurt. Father and the deacons kept watching the doors and windows. I wasn't sure of exactly what I was afraid of, but I knew that I should be.

The shakiness of fear cut through every conversation that tried to be had. The men uneasily danced around topics, trying to keep me from understanding the adult talk they were having. The aroma of the coffee presented the illusion of home and family and gave off a sense of awkwardness at the same time.

The only sense of ease came from Deacon Hall. His arms rested on the arms of his chair. His face was resigned and without emotion. In between the honking of the horn and the yelping of the sirens his eyes went to another place or another time. And when he returned, he had answers to the problem of the Negroes in America, all followed by a light, "God willing."

Father drank in everything that Deacon Hall was saying. Right before my eyes, he became a little boy looking to his father, Deacon Hall, for guidance. I wanted to tell on him. I wanted to tell Deacon Hall that Father had been misbehaving. I wanted to tell how he hit mother, and what Cyndi had said about him making Sister Jesse say hallelujah. In between the noise, I wanted to tell.

Deacon Henson jumped with each honk of the horn. His temples moved in and out with the grinding motion of his teeth from side to side. Had he screamed, I would not have been surprised.

"What do they want?" It seemed like Father was looking up at Deacon Hall when he asked the question. His hands flailed in the air and then rubbed his thighs.

"They just trying to scare you is all."

"And they gonna keep on, 'til they know for sure you scared." Deacon Henson sat at the edge of his chair. He rested his elbows on his knees and looked down at the floor. "They want to make sure you know your place. Negroes around here don't act up. They stay in their place. They get their heads knocked in and still stay in their place."

Deacon Hall interrupted, "You ought not speak that way in the presence of women folk. Besides, it ain't all of that. We don't have much trouble in these parts."

"We don't have much trouble cause we ain't doing nothing. Long as they think you scared, you don't ever have to see 'em. That's why we ain't got much trouble. They knows all the Negroes around here is scared!" Deacon Henson leaned back, and wiped his sweaty forehead with the palm of his right hand.

Father sat staring at the door. Our breathing seemed to echo throughout the room. There were no horns or sirens. Everything got quiet. We sat there looking at one another.

Knock!Knock!Knock! There were three swift knocks on the front door. Like he was the visitor, Father looked at Deacon Hall, who in turn nodded towards the door. Knock, knock,

knock! They came again. Father pushed himself up from the chair and steadied himself against the arm. He opened the door slightly, and I could see a white face press inward.

"Good evening, officer." Father spoke softly, but clearly.

"Evening?" The officer pushed the door open and stepped inside, revealing another officer leaning against the railing of our porch. "You boys didn't hear us beckoning for you to come outside?"

"Evenin' Sheriff." Deacon Hall stepped in between Father and the officer. "You need us sir?"

"Julius, we heard it was some niggers 'round here, tending to make some trouble for us. We was just wonderin' if ya'll done heard anything 'bout that. You know we ain't much for trouble around here."

"Naw sir, I ain't heard nothin' bout that. We was just getting our new Revun settled in." Deacon Hall's shoulders were hunched and both hands were in his pockets as he looked down at the rug. Deacon Henson, stayed seated and made no eye contact with anyone. His temples moved more quickly now than they had before.

"Yep, Julius, you one of the good ones. So boy, you the new preacher, huh? We hear you ain't from around these parts. Well, we don't put up with all that foolishness them Yankees up north put up with." Father stood stiffly. His back and neck straight. He had a slight grin on his face, like he shared a secret only him and the sheriff knew.

"I am not here to make any trouble for you sheriff."

"You not one of them fucking marching niggers is you?"

Father stood motionless. He had threatened to throw Uncle Byrd out on the street for less offensive talk.

"You hear me talking to you boy?" The sheriff had moved around Deacon Hall and was now standing face-to-face with Father. A lump in my throat tightened and I started to cough. Mama lay my head in her lap and rubbed my back, then my head, then my back again.

"Yes, I hear you and I assure you that I did not come to make any trouble."

"What kind of talk is that for a nigger? You one of those uppity ones, huh? Seem like we may have to teach you a thing or two. In these parts, you say 'yes sir', you hear?" The sheriff stepped closer to Father, if that was at all possible. Mother pushed my head out of her lap.

She leaped up from the sofa and ran over to Father. She grabbed his arm and slid in between him and the sheriff.

"Yes sir," she panted. "Yes, sir. We understand." Father shook her hand away from his arm. The sheriff grinned a grin that made me start to cry again.

"Julius, it's a little late for you boys to be out. Maybe you should be heading home now." The sheriff looked back at Deacon Hall and then over to Deacon Henson who hadn't moved.

"Yessir," Deacon Hall said. "We was just leaving anyhow. Come on Tommy, let's let the Revun' get some rest now." Tommy moved quickly from the seat and out the door without saying a word.

"Yes, 'revun,'" the sheriff said mockingly. "You get some rest now, you hear?" He and the other officer laughed as they walked down the steps.

Father closed the door when he heard the car doors slam.

"Will they be okay, Herb?" Mama asked about the deacons. He quickly drew back his hand and slapped her. The lick sent her tumbling to the ground. Its sound seemed louder than the horn and the sirens had.

"Don't you ever speak for me!" Father growled through his clinched teeth. He stood straddled over mama. "You ain't no man!"

A single tear fell from his cheek onto mama's forehead as he kicked her in the side.

"I'm the man." He mumbled trying to convince himself.

A warmth moved from my stomach, to my chest, and into my mouth. I leaned over the side of the couch and vomited.

Father's reddened eyes turned towards me and I heaved again.

"Get her!" He ordered mama. Stepping heavily, he went down the hall and into their bedroom. "Damn devil!" he slammed the door behind him.

I already knew everything about the church building. It rested right where my dream had left it, in the middle of the ring of towering trees. It had three rooms and was painted white, just the same as my dream. Deacon Hall and a thick smell of gas and wet wood met us at the doorway when we arrived.

"We jes' finishin da Sunday school lessons." He tipped his hat to Mama, smiled a wide grin for me, and shook Father's hand all before any of us had a chance to even speak. He, I thought, was what my own grandfather was really like. He was warm and playful and I could see myself in him and he didn't mind. He flicked his head as direction for us to follow him.

He showed Father to the pastor study. His study. It was the same size as mama's broom closet at the new house, but there was a desk, chair, and a lamp. It smelled wet.

"You jes set yo belongings there and rest ya self." Traces of red dirt gathered around the cuffs of Deacon Hall's brown pants which didn't match his green, yellow, and red plaid jacket. Deacon Hall's grin hadn't gotten any smaller even with Father's frown. "Take ya time and make ready. I'll come for ya when service done got on the way. You need any thang jes peek ya head out heah and Ill see ya fa sho." Deacon Hall took Father's coat and hung it on the hook fixed to the door.

"Now, ladies you jes follow me and I'll show you the rest of our humble abode." Deacon Hall bowed and put his hand out ushering us past him, play-acting like we were royalty.

The sanctuary, a perfect square, was the only room that could hold more than three people at a time. Two unpainted wood steps led to the two-pew choir stand that was directly behind the pulpit where Father would sit straight-backed and wide-legged.

The pews, painted caramel-brown, were made of six wood planks – three at the bottom and three at the back- that came together in the shape of an L. Wide hips hung over the three planks at the bottom. The longest pews were for the congregation. Faced forward, they stretched from one side of the church to the other and left only a narrow walkway between the ends of the pews and the walls. A wobbly dark brown offering table and a few feet separated the congregation from the pulpit. Four shorter pews, for the deacons and their wives, were at the front of the church. The deacons sat in the two that were to the right of the pulpit, and the two to the left were for their wives. With the backs of the pews towards the outer walls, the deacons and the deaconesses could watch both the pulpit and the congregation.

Somehow, the dream that I had had a week ago had leapt out of my mind and become real. The mahogany upright piano, situated against the right wall of the choirs stand, the two space-heaters, one between the Deacon's pew and the congregation and the other between the Deaconess's pew and the congregation, and the uncovered light fixture hanging from the ceiling above the pulpit were exactly as I remembered them. The power of knowing sent twinges of excitement through.

Deacon Hall showed us to our seats in the front pew closer to the side with the Deaconesses.

Sunday school let out and the pews filled up. As people came, the chill from the door opening and closing covered the warmth from the space-heaters. I shivered with my coat laying beside me. No one else had their coat on inside the church.

"Guide me over, thy great Jehovah. Pilgrim through this barren land."

Service began with a hymn. Deacon Henson stood at the front of the church next to the offering table and bellowed the words of the song, calling to the congregation. His deep voice was a little raspy but very powerful. The congregation poured out their voices in response to his call. The sound was both rich and mournful at the same time. Looking around, I saw hands and faces lifted towards God. Some had their eyes closed. Some, with open eyes, seemed as if they were looking through the roof of the church straight into heaven and were pleading with God. The weight of their voices pressed on my heart, and I lifted my hands toward heaven too.

"I am weak, but thou art mighty. Hold me with thine powerful hand."

Deacon Henson nodded his head, handing the service over to Deacon Hall who knelt down in front of the deacon's pew. The congregation took the queue, lowered their singing to a moan, and bowed their heads. Deacon Hall's voice lifted and fell with prayer, blanketing the small church. Mountaintops and valleys, he covered them all with his praise and his pleas. Part of the congregation continued to hum as others supported Deacon Hall with "Do Lawds", "Yes sirs", and "Amens."

"And Lawd, don't forget to bless our new pastor and wife and their beautiful daughter. We thank ya for sending em this way. Fuh what is a sheep without a shepherd? Lawd have mercy on our souls...," Deacon Hall prayed.

When he said 'Amen,' I lifted my head higher than it had ever been before. I was wrapped up in the word beautiful.

After devotion, Sister Carter stood to give the church announcements.

"We so pleased wit havin our new revun wit us here today," she smiled. "Other than dat, it ain't much in the way of new 'nouncements. Women be mindful of Women in White program. We'll talk more on that at Mission meetin on Tuesday night. Thank ya," she nodded to Deacon Hall and settled back into her seat.

As soon as she had finished, the choir stood, and a woman who had been sitting with the deacon's wives climbed the steps and crossed the choir stand over to the piano. She was not much taller than myself, but her weighty flesh overpowered her short frame, making her sway from side to side as she trudged along. When she sat down at the piano her fingers began to flow over the keys. The music streaming from the old piano and this woman drew me into a beautiful place inside my mind. The choir swayed with the music, and at just the right time, they started singing. People in the congregation began to pop up out of their seats, clapping and swaying and singing along, the atmosphere was charged with a power that was hard to ignore.

After the first song, a tall slender lady in a canary yellow dress stepped down from the

second pew of the choir-stand to the first.
Deacon Hall scrambled from his seat to hand
her the microphone from the pulpit, where
Father sat wide-legged and straight-backed. His
brown suit was neatly pressed and his shoes
freshly shined. He didn't look like any of the
other men in the church, many who had simply
worn a suit jacket over their coveralls. Their
faces were hard and worn, but pleasant. In their
laps, they held fedoras that had covered their
short kinky hair. Father hadn't worn a hat to
cover his conked hair.

"Amazing grace, how sweet the sound.
That saved a wretch like me. I once was lost,
but now, I'm found. Was blind, but now I see."

Her high soprano voice was better than
people I'd heard on the radio. She didn't really
need a microphone, her voice was so strong and
clear, and I felt Mama's body stiffen beside me.
I looked up at her just as she was dabbing the
tear from her cheek with her handkerchief.
While the woman sang, Deacon Hall and
another man from one of the deacon's pews
walked down the aisles passing the offering
plates. By the time the lady finished the song,
all of the offering had been collected and Father
was standing behind the podium in the pulpit,

opening his Bible. The entire congregation stood to their feet in acknowledgement.

"Glory be to God. Who is the alpha and the omega." Father's opening words were the same ones that Reverend Johanson, the pastor of our church in Chicago, said each time he started his sermon. Father said them proudly, as if they were his own. The lull of soft sounds of the piano carried his words.

"I am pleased and humbled to be the pastor of True Mount Baptist Church." He reached into the pocket inside his suit jacket and pulled out the reading glasses that he had bought from Woolworth's just before we moved to Texas. He had good eyesight, but thought they made him look distinguished. They were round with gold rims. A black owl, I thought. I imagined Father hooting, lowered my eyes and smiled at my Bible as I waited for Father to give the scripture.

"If you would, turn in your Bibles to Daniel, chapter 3 beginning with verse 16." Pages rattled as some of the congregation flipped through their Bibles, while others stood holding their closed Bibles in front of them, simply nodding. The congregation settled into their seats after Father read the scripture, but soon began to pop up again, shouting, "Go 'head preacher", and "Amen", and waving their hands in the air. When Father reached the height of his sermon, the musician started accompanying his words with music from the piano.

"Be still," Mama leaned over and whispered to me. When I couldn't stop my legs from swinging, she pressed her gloved hand into my thigh and shot me a look that made everything be still. Rouge covered the slight purple bruise on her cheek, and she was beautiful. Her gloved hands rested neatly in her lap. Her knees were pressed tightly together and her legs were crossed at the ankle.

"But Shadrach, Meshach, and Abednego would not bow down!" Father's rolling voice filled the small church. His smooth black face was covered with sweat that collected around his shirt collar. Deacon Hall passed him a white handkerchief.

"You can laugh at me… you can talk about me…you can even put me in the pit of fire! Even then…I said even then…I will have no other gods before my God. So, if you put me in the fire…,God's will be done. Though they slay me…yet will I trust in my God."

Father moved back and forth across the pulpit as he preached, getting louder and more excited as he went on.

"God can! God can! My God can! Deliver me." Father slapped the wooden podium harder each time he said it. Nearing the end of his sermon, he was now sing-preaching, the words rolling out together and forming spontaneous song. It wasn't hard to put pictures to the stories Uncle Byrd told about Father singing in the Black clubs around Chicago. His voice was so smooth and rich.

The way Uncle Byrd said it always made me giggle, "He was a cool cat." He would stretch out "coooooool" and slide his hand slowly around his head stroking the brim of an imaginary hat.

"He drew the women like bees to honey. Them singin' negroes always could do that." Then Uncle Byrd would let out an open-mouthed laugh and slap his thigh. He was quick to explain that he never had any trouble with the women himself, but that his luck was all due to good looks cause he couldn't carry a tune in a bucket.

Sometimes Father himself would laugh a little at Uncle Byrd's stories, but he never joined in the telling.

"Yep, that's how he met that pretty little Bea. Stole her right from under my nose." Uncle Byrd would shoot a sly look over at mama who would always blushingly lower her eyes and turn away. By the time Uncle Byrd would get to the part about how the preacher came into one of the joints Father was singing at and "discovered" him, Father would have gotten tired of the story and would tell Uncle Byrd to shut up with all his lies. Uncle Byrd said that that preacher was the slickest thing he'd ever seen in a club and dressed sharper than a tack.

"HE MAY NOT COME WHEN YOU WANT HIM, huh, BUT HE'S ALWAYS......huh.....ALWAYS.........huh... ....ALWAYS..........ON TIME!" I could feel Father's voice tumbling around inside my chest. The entire congregation were on their feet, waving their hands and shouting their, "Yea Lawds", "Go heads", and "Preach Revuns!"

One of the deacon's wives let out a yelping screech. Her body folded and unfolded as she jerked forward and then back.

"Hallelujah!" she jumped up out of her seat and took off running down the aisle. Nothing like this had ever happened at our church at home. An usher would have come and politely tapped on shoulders and whispered in ears. Nothing like this could have ever happened, but I knew exactly what it was. And I liked it.

Four other church women caught the Holy Ghost and danced and shouted their ways from between the pews out into the aisles. The musician played the piano furiously. The congregation kept the fast beat with handclaps and stomping feet. The shouting women jumped up and down and ran back and forth, shuffling their feet in dance even faster than the quick-clapping hands. One of the deacons marched in place rubbing the sides of his thighs with the palms of his hands. Eyes closed, he didn't yell and scream like the women, but I knew he must have felt the same thing as they did. He just shook his head from side-to-side and rubbed his thighs.

I slid up to the edge of the pew and lowered my feet to the dusty wood floor. I could feel the vibrations of the shouting ladies through the soles of my Sunday shoes. The church was charged with the energy of these people, raggedy and all, praising God. I thought of standing, but glanced over at mama instead.

Satisfaction covered Father's face as he wiped away the sweat with the white handkerchief. He stood at the edge of the raised pulpit and lifted his right hand.

"If there are any, who don't know the Lord, Jesus Christ as your personal savior…don't be ashamed. Give your life to Christ today. He is here and he's waiting for you! I wouldn't die and go to hell if I were you."

The choir sang softly as Father waited to see if anyone had gotten up from their seats and started down the aisle towards him. *Come, come to Jesus while you have time. Come, come to Jesus make up your mind.* Their voices blended together perfectly.

"Don't let the devil stay in your life. Put him out! He may stop by, but don't let him stay!"

Everything stopped for me including my breath. I waited to see if his face would turn into that of a snake like it had in my dream. Nothing happened.

Two women and a little boy gave their lives to Christ and joined church. Six others, backsliders, went down to the alter to give their lives back to Christ and the church again.

After service, Father stood next to the offering table, shaking hands and accepting compliments. Some of the women pulled Mama aside and told her about Mission Society, and the upcoming Women in White program. I inched my way to the pew closest to the door where some of the other kids were waiting.

"That's a pretty dress," a girl reached out her hand, sticky with the peppermint candy that she had just stuck back into her mouth, and felt the hem of my navy blue velveteen dress.

"Thank you. I'm Ruthie."

"Yeah, you da revun's lil girl."

"How old is you?" The boy, slightly taller than myself, poked me in the arm as he asked. I had pretended he had nothing to do with my inching to the back pew, but I had seen him mimicking Father while he was preaching and knew I wanted to meet him.

"Teddy, you do-do head! She ain't even talkin' to you. Go on now!" The girl stood up from the bench and pushed the boy on his shoulder. She was protecting me.

"My name Theodore. Theodore Hall." And he feigned a chivalrous bow.

"Teddy, ain't nobody studyin' you. Go on and leave her alone."

"Ten. I'm ten." I finally got it out.

"Ya'll rich?" Teddy ignored the girl and felt the sleeve of my dress.

"No, we're not rich."

"Ya'll from up nawth ain't ya? You rich. You can tell me." Teddy's grin was warm and sly at the same time.

"She ain't got to tell you nothin." The girl had placed herself in between me and Teddy.

"Teddy and Madeline sittin' in a tree. K-I-S-S-I-N-G." Two other girls, watching from the pew, covered their mouths with their hands and sang only loud enough for us kids to hear.

"Don't try me," Madeline rolled her eyes and put her hands on her hips. The girls stopped singing, but the giggles kept going.

Madeline turned back towards me. My first thought was to run. "Who ya'll gonna eat dinner with?" She must've seen the confusion on my face, "The preacher always eat Sunday dinner at somebody's house. Who ya'll eating with?

"I don't know."

"Oh." We stood there for a while, just looking at one another. Teddy was gone and the other kids had lost interest.

"Come on Ruthie, let's go." Mama touched my shoulder as she passed.

"Bye," I said faintly and waived at Madeline.

Father laughed and talked all the way home. Mama just kept on and on about how well he had preached and how the Spirit really showed up. Twice, she reached over and rubbed his back. Even I grinned and chatted a bit. At least ten people had said how pretty I was in my dress. They filled my hands with pieces of butterscotch and peppermint.

The crisp pine air blanketed me. Chicago was far away and that was fine. Father had brought me to people who loved me, people who thought I was pretty, not "more ugly," and smart. I actually liked him at this moment. I pressed my cheek against the cool window and looked at the towering trees along the highway. Today they were beautiful.

"And boy can that Sister Wright sing or what?" Father disappeared into a distant memory. He was talking about the woman who had sung "Amazing Grace" before he started his sermon. With her cropped hairstyle and tight-fitting yellow dress, she seemed more like one of the Supremes than a church singer. "Sweeter than a hummingbird, her voice was. Full of honey," Father said, but not to us. He drew himself into some distant place where him and his own thoughts were the only things that were important. Mama turned and stared out the window, and Father didn't come back to us until we made it home.

At dinner, he went on and on about what he would do at his church. And how he was going to turn these back-wood hicks around.

"When I get through here, you won't have seen a better church. Bea, you know that big fancy one on 19ᵗʰ street in Chicago… Reverend Hawkins' church? Mine will top that one ten times over."

Mama smiled a stupidly gracious smile and picked at her food.

When he stopped talking long enough to fill his mouth with chicken and peas, I asked, "Why we didn't go to one of the member's houses for dinner?"

He looked up from his plate and frowned at me. "Why you ask that?"

"Madeline said that the preacher always eats Sunday dinner with one of the families in the church."

"We are not going to go around eating squirrel or possum or whatever they're having these days. These monkeys up here don't know nothing about being civilized. No telling what they'd try to feed me."

"Herbert," Mama said with a heavy breath.

"Don't Herbert me. I'm not going to sugar coat it for her. You stay away from those little dirty ninnies. They don't have good manners and I'm not sure how clean they are."

Mama got up from the table with her plate. "People can't always help the state they're in," she barely mumbled as she scraped what was left of her dinner into the trash.

"Howdy revun. Mawnin' revun. How you be today?" Father said with a slow, thick drawl mocking the church members. "Bunch of back-road niggers is all they are." He laughed at his own imitations of the congregation.oo

I thought about Madeline and how she had said how pretty my dress was and how she was ready to protect me. Her dress had been old, but it was clean. Too much of her long black legs had showed from beneath the faded dress. Her hair hadn't been press-combed so it hardly came together in the ponytails. I thought about Curtis and how his black socks showed from beneath his blue pants. I thought about the church people with whom Father had grinned and shook hands, gladly taking their offering money. They had patted my head. To them, I wasn't ugly or different. I was normal, and to some, even special. My heartbeat started racing and my fingers tightened around the handle of my fork. A deep heat moved beneath my skin. I felt the same way about Father as I had about dirty gap-toothed Carl Brown. I wondered how I had looked on top of him pounding him with my fists and then trying to scratch his eyes out.

"Wipe that smirk off your face," Father shouted at me. "You've got about as much sense as a bessie-bug sitting their grinning like you crazy." I hadn't even noticed that I was almost smiling. In my mind, he was Carl.

CHAPTER

14

The sign said, "A. Lincoln Primary School – Colored." Mama drove me. She had made me change clothes twice.

"Are you trying to look like a ragamuffin?" She had asked the second time I went into the kitchen. "You can't go around looking any kind of way. Your Father…," for a second, she seemed to be looking past me. "Go back in there and change. I'm just gonna have to get rid of that stuff since you don't have the sense God gave you not to wear it."

What was good enough for me to wear in Chicago wasn't good enough here in the pine woods and red dirt. My plaid skirt was my favorite, so when I pulled it off I stuffed it between my mattresses just in case mama really decided to get rid of some of my things. There were only a few things left to choose from, so I put on my orange pleated skirt and kept on the yellow blouse. At least now my yellow-and-orange striped knee-hi socks matched.

When the car stopped, mama sat there with both her hands locked on the steering wheel. "Mind your manners Ruthie, and I will pick you up when school lets out." I sat there waiting for something else, but that was it.

The school was a long, wood building with dirty yellow paint. There wasn't any sidewalk leading up to the front door, only a trail. The yard was small patches of grass surrounded by red dirt and rocks.

I got out of the car and followed some of the other kids into the long wood building. All of the doors to the classrooms had signs posted, Grade 1, Grade 2, and so on. I walked down the narrow hallway until I saw Grade 4. A tall, slender lady with small round glasses and her hair pulled back into a bun was about to close the door just as I walked up.

"Good morning. You must be Ruthie, come on in." Her voice was warm. Her words were crisp not long and drawn-out like the other people here in Billings. "Class, we have a new student, her name is Ruthie Johnson." She must have been from somewhere else.

"Good morning, Ruthie," the class said in one voice.

"Ruthie, you can sit here beside Sara Jane," the lady pointed to a seat in the front row.

"Everyone, we will go down each row. Tell Ruthie your name." When they were all done, I thought to myself that I should have told her to call me Ruthie Ann. Most of the other kids went by two names. I wondered if it were too late to change and tell her to call me Ruthie Ann. The more I tried to decide whether or not to tell her, the faster my heart beat.

"And I'm Ms. Bayard. I'm sure you all will take some special time today to properly welcome Ruthie and make her feel right at home," she eyed the rest of the class and then gave me a reassuring smile. "Now, take out your readers and turn to page 68." My heart calmed down a little, because now it was too late to tell her. She had moved on. Everyone opened their desktops and pulled out their books.

"Ruthie, your reader is in your desk." Ms. Bayard looked at me from over the top of her glasses. There were three books inside, neither was new. "I will get book covers for you after lunch. I'm sure, I don't have to tell you how important it is to take care of your books. That means no markings and such."

I nodded and pulled out my reader. I would never mark in my books anyway. The cover was torn and pages had already been marked. "This book belongs to Suzanne Nichols" was written across the top of the first page.

I raised my hand.

"Yes, Ruthie."

"I think this is someone else's book. It's already been written in."

Kids giggled all around me. Were they laughing at the way I talked? I shrunk a little.

Ms. Bayard sighed, "No, Ruthie. That is your book. Now turn to page 68 please. Judy, start reading at the top of the page." The girl stood beside her desk and started to read aloud. I slumped down in my chair and followed along.

When it was time to study science, Ms. Bayard told us to choose partners.

"Ruthie, you be my partner," Madeline grabbed my hand. I hadn't noticed her sitting in the back of the class.

"No, she's with me," Sara Jane pulled my other hand as two other girls came to claim me as their partner. I looked from girl to girl. This would have never been a problem in Chicago.

"Girls!" Ms. Bayard came over and began to send them away, leaving me with Madeline who chose a table near the window for us to work at. A slight stream of air flowed inside even though the window was shut.

The assignment was to shape a volcano out of the red clay dirt that had been gathered from outside. Each table had a pile of dirt, a cup of water, and a Popsicle stick. I could see that ours had come from a red one.

"Careful not to add too much water," Ms. Bayard instructed from the front of the classroom.

"You like it down heah?" Madeline stuck her hand in the cup and let the water drip from her fingers onto the pile of dirt.

"Yes, I like it fine."

"What's it like up where you from? You seen the statue of liberty?"

"No, that's in New York. I'm from Chicago." Madeline lowered her eyes. "But one day I'll see it." I smiled at her, and she smiled back, her teeth pale yellow.

"Me too. I'm gonna go see it too."

Glancing out of the window, I saw a red pickup truck pull into the school yard. It was a white man. Not like the ghosts at the bus depot. He was real. Four big barrels showed over the sides of the truck's wagon. It seems like I was the only one who noticed because no one else stopped working to look. He stepped out of the truck and moved around to the back and let down the tailgate. Stepping up into the bed of the truck, he began to move the barrels closer to the edge.

"What is he doing?" I whispered to Madeline, trying to hide my alarm.

"Who?"

"That man. Out there in the truck." Madeline looked up from the clay and in the direction my finger was pointing.

"Quit pointin' else you have bad luck," she said, matter-of-factly. She must have read the confused look on my face. "Pointin' at white folks," she explained, "give you bad luck. You end up losin a finger." I stared at her to see if she was joking, but there was no trace of a smile.

"Ya'll don't have lunch up there where you from?"

"Lunch?"

"Uh hum. Lunch."

"I don't see any lunch." I leaned against the table with both hands palm down, tilted my head to the right, and looked Madeline straight in her eyes to let her know I was no fool. She stopped shaping the clay and looked at me seriously.

"Okay, see those barrels?" She nodded her head, but did not point. "Well, they bring those over from the white school. And then they po 'em up into those big black pans for when we go into the lunchroom," she had started back shaping the clay.

Ms. Bayard shook the silver bell that had been on the corner of her desk. "I'm letting you go a little early so that you can stop by the washroom to wash your hands."

"Come on!" Madeline grabbed my hand and pulled me to the line that was beginning to form at the door of the classroom. "We don't wanna be last in line. The quicker you get your food and eat, the more time you have to play outside."

"Chocolate milk 2 for $.05 or 1 for $.03."

The only sign in the lunchroom grabbed my attention. The food was in big black pans, just like Madeline had said. We rushed through our mashed potatoes and meatloaf without much conversation. Madeline hadn't let any of the other girls join us.

Outside, there were kids from the fourth, fifth, and sixth grade classes. One slide stood at the center of the playground, which was mostly rocks and dirt. Kids stood in line for minutes before getting a chance to climb the slide's ladder. Some ran around playing freeze tag. I stood in the center of a circle of girls answering questions and smiling, making sure that they knew that I was one of them. Madeline stood next to me and pushed anyone away who she thought asked a silly question.

I am sitting on the top branch of a huge tree in the middle of an open field. The wind smells like dead animals. I know it's me even though I am looking down at myself sitting there. A snow white coyote is looking up at me from the trunk of the tree. I look over to the right and see a giant snake with black scales wearing a golden crown. It is standing upright like before the fall of Adam. It opens its mouth and I can see the fangs. They're huge, even from where I'm sitting. There's a little girl in a white dress. When she turns around she sees the snake, I see her face. It is mama, and her eyes are dark, round, and unblinking like a baby doll's. The snake gulps her up with one bite, turns and looks at me and smiles. My heart pounds with anger because she didn't try to fight. When I look to my left I see a white church burning. People are standing in line with buckets

*in their hands but they are just looking at one another.
No one is trying to put out the fire. Teddy is there, and
Madeline, and some of the other girls from school, and
even Carl Brown. Then the snake starts to head over to
the church. I jump from the tree and land on all fours
like an animal and I roar. The snake looks at me and
laughs. When I stand upright, I am naked. I run
towards the snake. The closer I get to it the bigger it gets.
My heart is racing, but I am not afraid. I just know
that I have to get to the snake before he gets to the
church. If not, the people will turn around and see that
I am naked. I haunch on all fours and then leap from
the ground. My fingers are blades and I use them to slice
his head away from his body. Then the people turn
towards me and smile. I am not naked.*

"What you starin' at?" Madeline reminded me a
lot of Cyndi.

"I ain't staring. Your hair bow is pretty,
but it's about to fall off."

"Thanks girl."

I dream a lot now. Sometimes, I am not
even asleep when I am dreaming. Sometimes,
the dreams play out above people's heads. I try
to blink them away, but they keep playing. Last

Sunday, I saw a baby boy over Sister Wright's head. He was dark brown with chubby legs. On his left thigh, he had a birthmark like Father's. One time, I saw Deacon Hall turn into me and then back into himself. And I saw Deacon Henson
touch a white woman's titties.

The first time they came to the church was a Wednesday night Bible study and we had stopped the service. This time we kept right on singing over the howling sirens.

Madeline and Teddy and any of the other kids who didn't have to sit with their mother or grandmother during service had taken to sitting on the second pew with me since I couldn't sit in the back of the church with them. So that Wednesday when the sirens first came, I was sitting between Madeline and mama as still as everything else inside the church.

Deacon Hall had been the first to move. With one quick hand motion and head nod, he signaled for Father and another brother to follow him, and for Deacon Henson to go to Father's study.

Deacon Hall and the steel-gray coyote that only I could see, were the first ones outside the church. They were the last to come back inside, seeming led by Father and then the other brother, but I knew that they were still leading. Inside the church, nothing changed, until Deacon Hall closed the door and signaled for Sister Mavis to start playing the piano again and the rest of the service picked up from there.

The second time the sirens came was a lot like the first only Deacon Henson was not there.

The first time, Teddy was the first one to see the scarecrow hanging from the tree after service.

"Do Lord, do Lord." I heard two of the sisters whispering from behind their hands, covering their mouths.

"Be damned," a man's voice.

"Lawdy be."

"What they do this for?"

"What we gonna do?"

"Do Lord."

"Mercy Jesus."

Now, everyone was looking at the scarecrow that Teddy hadn't stopped pointing at since he first discovered it.

Mama was squeezing the breath out of me, until I finally freed myself from her arms wrapped around my shoulders and chest. She stood behind me with nothing to do with her newly freed arms. They could not reach for Father standing at her side.

"Revun," Deacon Hall leaned in close to Father, "I spectin' you better say somethin' or you goin' to lose these here people. I'll follow you."

Father raised both his hands. "This, see this is the devil's work. But we, we are the children of God. And if we just…," he got louder as he went on and all of the mumbling faded away, "trust in God, everything is going to be alright. This is the house of the Lord, but it is not exempt from the wiles of the devil. Yes, he may even stop by here, but he surely won't stay." Father grew bigger and bigger. "Now, you all just pack up and go on home. Don't worry because God is with you."

There was a long silence before people began to shuffle away. With the sounds of movement, Deacon Henson stepped in and added, "If we could get a few men to hang around and help us for a coupla' minutes, be mighty obliged."

Father shrank, but not before Deacon Henson gave him a respectful nod, hat in hand.

That was the night that Father beat mama so badly that she had to stay home from church for two whole weeks. When Madeline asked me if she was sick, I said, "Yes, but not too sick."

This time, we just kept on singing.

Sister Wright was the first one to see it. She didn't sit in the choir stand anymore since her stomach started getting big. Now she sat at the back of the church. Madeline said it wouldn't be long before she didn't come at all since she didn't have a husband and she was getting fat and all.

"I ain't gonna be eatin' no watermelon seeds 'for I have a husband," Madeline smacked her lips and confided in the group of us girls standing in a circle outside of the church. I knew that she was talking about Sister Wright, because she was cutting her eyes towards her.

"What does watermelon seeds have to do with anything?" As soon as I asked, she pulled me aside from the rest of the group.

"Girl, you don't know? If you swallow watermelon seeds, then your stomach swells up all big and stuff and if you ain't married it's a dis...grace. Yeah, a disgrace."

I had to blink back my disbelief. "Madeline, that is not a watermelon, she is going to have a baby."

"I know that! That's what I'm sayin'."

"A baby don't come from watermelon seeds!"

"They don't come from watermelon seeds, that's how you make 'em."

"Madeline, a baby comes from when a man puts his thing inside a woman vagina and then they have a baby." Madeline's mouth flew open and stayed that way for a long five seconds, before she threatened to tell on me for talking nasty. I caught her arm just as she was turning to run off and gave her half of my Chic-O-Stic. I made her promise not to tell, and I promised her that I would show her in a real book that what I said was true.

After service, people were gathering their things. Women were talking about the greens and chicken and fresh biscuits and dumplings and desserts that they had thrown together for Sunday supper, when Sister Wright's scream tore through the thick layer of chatter.

Outside the church, in the same big elm that the scarecrow had hung from on that Wednesday night, Deacon Henson's body swayed from side-to-side with the breeze.

I never saw a dead person before. I'd seen a dead dog. His eyes were open and his mouth. His stomach was stretched tight and big even though his legs were flattened to the hot tar. And he stank. Not like need-a-bath stink, but like meat-rotting-when-the-electricity-is-out stink.

It looked like Deacon Henson was looking at us over his right shoulder, but I knew he was dead, dangling from the limb like some strange fruit ready to fall to the ground. His body was surrounded by darkness with the moon as his spotlight. It was a full moon. His hands were tied behind his back and his pants were gathered around his ankles. Something, maybe an apron, was tied around his waist. I could hear what death sounded like. I understood what Mahalia Jackson meant when she sang, "no more, no more weeping and 'a wailing." It's different from crying. Crying comes from the heart, what I heard came from the stomach.

"Jesus," one of the sisters cried out. Some of the women fell to the ground into the red dirt.

"Why Lord? Why?" I kept hearing over. "This ain't s'pose to happen no more. This ain't s'pose to happen!"

People shuffled hurriedly to nowhere and then back again. Mothers grabbed children and tried to cover their eyes. Men walked quickly, sometimes ran. They looked down, searching for something to put into their hands. Some found sticks others found rocks. Families gathered together and then moved apart again. Someone tried to turn my face away from Deacon Henson. They couldn't move me. A man was hanging from a tree. Women covered their faces. Men lowered their heads in shame. Deacon Henson had given me peppermint. People began to bump into one another, moving nowhere quickly. Tears warmed my face, but I still did not turn away. People frantically gathered their Bibles and their children and their husbands and wives. I could't cry. The air was too dense. It was hard for me to breathe. But I still couldn't turn away. No goodbyes or "you have a good evenin' ya hear?" Only a few, "be carefuls." People scurried towards the few cars and piled in. The crunching sound of tires against the gravelly rocks of the dirt road ripped through the air. Families who usually walked to church accepted rides in the backs of pickup trucks. It was an evacuation with no sirens only a body hanging from a tree. "I told him to leave that white girl alone," Deacon Hall spoke to no one and everybody at the same time. His words rested heavily on my shoulder.

"Is yo mama white?" Sara Jane had asked me on my first day of school.

"You so dumb, her mama ain't white!" Madeline pushed her out of the circle that had gathered around me.

"The Lord giveth and the Lord taketh away." The Bible didn't mean it the way the preachers and church folks said it. They said it like God came down and took something from us. They said it like, He wanted it more that we did and since He was the biggest and baddest, he just came and took it...like He was a bully. Father said it like the white folks didn't have anything to do with this. At least he didn't talk about God picking flowers this time. Deacon Henson wasn't a flower and God didn't pick him to take him to heaven. I took a deep breath and remembered the smell of peppermint that always seemed to float around Deacon Henson. I knew I was right; he wasn't a flower.

Father led the procession of other preachers, deacons, and Deacon Henson's family members into the church. The first two rows on each side of the aisle had been roped off for the deacons and Deacon Henson's family. We hadn't really needed any rope because the church was only about half full. The preachers bunched together in the pulpit. They were mostly big men in black suits with white shirts. Most of them had hats resting in their laps or near their feet. Their hair was cut so short that you couldn't tell it was nappy. All of them, except the oldest preacher, had parts in their short cuts - some on the left, a couple on the right, and one right down the middle. They were packed in the pulpit so tightly, that they seemed to have melted into one another. There were plenty of empty seats in the congregation, but they all sat where they could be respected.

<u>Walk with me, Lord. Walk with me. Walk with me, Lord. Walk with me. While I'm on this, tedious journey. I need Jesus, to walk with me</u>. The woman sang with no music. Our musician didn't come to the funeral. There was more than half of our congregation missing.

"We are men, jes like them! And we deserve to be treated like men." The young preacher pounded the podium with each word. He'd been asked to read the scripture from the New Testament. It seemed like he had rushed through John 3:16, so that he could say just what he was saying. No one said amen, except for Deacon Hall. One family - a man, a woman, and a little girl - gathered their things and left the funeral.

"Jes preach the word, son," one of the older preachers mumbled from behind his crisp, white handkerchief as he tugged the younger preacher's coattail. The young preacher shook his head as he returned to his seat in the overcrowded pulpit.

When it was time for Father to deliver the eulogy, he rose up slowly as if he didn't really want to go to the podium. His face seemed a tight mix between angry and worried. He looked over at Deacon Hall and then down at the light blue casket that was in front of the pulpit. It seemed as if he was trying to look through the flowers that had been placed on top of the closed casket, through the blue paint, through the casket, and into the place where Deacon Henson's spirit had gone.

"It's awright, son. It's awright." The old preacher who had tugged on the younger one's coattail spoke again, but this time it was to Father. His words brought Father back to the funeral and back to the pulpit. He turned around and nodded respectfully to the old preacher.

"No sir, it is not alright. It is not alright." Then he began his sermon. I didn't hear it because I never got past, "It is not alright." After the service, Father, the younger preacher, and Deacon Hall disappeared into father's small office. I tried to rush Mama outside the church because I didn't want to stay inside with Deacon Henson's casket. They hadn't opened it during the funeral, but I knew he was inside. Finally, Mama let me go outside without her. I found Madeline as quickly as I could. Before I had a chance to say hello, she started talking.

"You know why they ain't gon' bury him, huh?" I guess my silence was enough to let Madeline know that I didn't know what she was talking about. I had wanted to show her the stickers that I had bought from the 5 and Dime in town. I had slipped them into my white, patent leather purse even though Mama had told me not to put anything inside but some tissues and a peppermint. She had said I didn't need to bring a purse and that I was acting too grown. Father had interrupted the scolding when he asked Mama to find his tie, the one with the red flecks. I slipped three of the stickers and a beaded necklace into my purse and set it on the porch, so I could easily pick it up without Mama knowing as we headed to the car.

"Why we ain't goin to the cemetery," Madeline's words were both a statement and a question. "Cause he was messin' round wit some white woman. That's why. That's why they killed him. He was dead 'fo they put him in the tree. He was already dead. The tree was for us. He was already dead." Madeline looked as if she could burst out crying at any time. I sat down on the tree stump beside her and we used small sticks to pick at the trail of ants that were parading in front of our feet.

18

Some of the members stopped coming to Wednesday night services after Deacon Henson was put up in the tree. Then when the police kept coming and blasting their sirens during the services, even more people stopped coming. They came Sunday mornings though. A little over a month after Deacon Henson and the sirens, Father stood in the pulpit. There were only nine of us there that night.

<u>Guide me o'er, thy Great Jehovah. Pilgrim through this barren land.</u> Deacon Hall knelt on one knee in front of the deacon's pew, head bowed, cupping his forehead in his right hand. Over the pew, I could see the bald spot in the center of his head surrounded by his tight gray hair. Now, it was only a little cool at night,

but he still wore the same thin brown and tan plaid coat that he had worn during the winter when we met him. He hadn't changed hats either. The flimsy brown felt one was on the pew next to him. He always took it off his head when he started climbing the church steps leading to the front door. He never wore it inside the church. Even in the rain, he took off his hat.

After we moved to Billings, Mama had bought me a maroon velvet coat with matching muffler trimmed in white fur, but she had made me stop wearing it at the end of January.

<u>I am weak but thou art mighty. Hold me with thou powerful hand</u>. Usually Deacon Hall's voice shook like when you sing in front of the fan. Sometimes at recess, Madeline would pretend that she was him, and she would make her voice sound gruff-like and hit really bad notes on purpose. Whoever was around laughed as if they had never seen her show before, even me. Teddy would act like he was mad, since it was his grandfather, but he laughed too.

Tonight was different.

<u>Bread of Heaven, bread of Heaven feed me til I want no more</u>. Deacon Hall's voice

ripped through the heavy air in the church. I could feel his words in my throat and in my chest.

"God has not given us the spirit of fear, but of power, and of love, and of a sound mind. We cannot go on like this Brothers and Sisters. We cannot let the devil keep us from serving our God. Now, God gave us a great commission. To go and tell this dying world that a Savior is come. How can we go tell the sinners to come when the saints don't even come?"

There were a few nods but no "amen."

"Are we going to let the devil stop us? No, we will not let him close these doors!"

Still no "amen."

Father slammed his hand hard against the podium. The sound bounced off of the four church walls. Nothing moved. Not until Father left the pulpit and went into his office.

The night before, Deacon Hall had stopped by our house, but he didn't come all of the way inside. He only stepped inside the door when he realized that he had interrupted dinner.

"So sorry revun. Don't know what I was thinkin comin this time u'tha night."

"Sure, sure Deacon. You know you're welcome here anytime…"

"Don't have good news revun," Deacon Hall cut in before Father could finish.

"Quit being grown and eat your food!" Mama tapped my hand when she saw that I had stopped eating and was straining to hear what was being said at the door. It was also a queue for Father and Deacon Hall, because after that I only heard whispers.

"Everything alright Herb?" Mama asked when Father came back to the table. "Why didn't you invite the deacon in for dinner?"

"Why you asking so many damned questions?"

"Herb, there's no need…"

"No need for what? Huh? No need for what? Who the hell are you to tell me what I do or do not need?"

"Herb, I was just."

"You need to be 'Just' shutting up. You the one in love with these niggers around here. I don't have to invite every Tom, Dick, and Harry in to my house for dinner."

"Herb," Mama dropped her head. I looked at her, but she did not look at me.

"Deacon Hall ain't a nigger." I looked at Father when Mama wouldn't.

"What did you say?" Father's fork clinked against his plate when he dropped it.

"Deacon Hall ain't a nigger."

"Listen to you, "ain't." You beginning to sound just like them. Girl, don't you ever, as long as you living and Black, sass me. I will beat the devil and spitfire out of you."

Father growled from between his cinched teeth. But I didn't look away. I didn't drop my head. Not because I wasn't afraid, but because of what I saw happening to his face. For a second, there would be scales like a snake covering his face and then he looked like a little boy with tears running down his chubby cheeks. And I thought of Sister Wright and the baby in her stomach. Then, he was Father again.

"Herbert, please." Mama spoke to her plate.

"Please what? Please the hell what?" Father picked up the piece of roast from his plate and threw it at Mama, hitting her in the face. When she jumped up, he did too, and his chair tumbled backwards. Its loud crash onto the linoleum was the bell that started the next round of fighting.

"Get out of here Ruthie!" Mama yelped at me after Father's second blow to her face, but before the next one to her stomach.

I walked, not ran, to my room and gently closed my door. From there, I did understand that fewer people in services meant less money to pay the church bills and less money to pay Father. He talked or shouted between delivering blows.

"Father God, in the name of Jesus we come bowed down befo' you humble as we know how." Tonight, when Deacon Hall prayed, I closed my eyes and prayed. And I saw faces in my head, mostly black, but some white. I saw babies and I felt sad. Then, I couldn't stop crying. Even when Mama told me to wipe my face cause I didn't have anything to be crying about, I couldn't stop crying. She pushed her boney yellow hand into my thigh. Pressed powder covered her Father-darkened eye and lipstick covered her busted lip, but she pressed her bone yellow hand into my thigh and said that I didn't have anything to be crying about. I opened my eyes to her stare and saw that the pressed powder was too light, and that you could still see the black eye.

Cover up your eye! I screamed at her in my mind. Cover up your eye! They're gonna see it and then they will talk about me.

"Look her momma got beat up," or, "What happened to your momma?" or, "Poor thing." "Poor little ugly black thing."

They like me here. I'm pretty here. Cover up your eye! I'm like them. I'm one of them. Cover up your eye!

Then, I fainted, and when I came to, I was laid out on the floor.

"Lawd ha'mercy!"

"Lawdy be, the Holy Ghost done got a hold of this child."

"Lawd ha'mercy! Use her Lawd cause she one of your'ne."

The handful of women, except for Mama, swarmed around me, praying and singing and praising God. I saw Father behind them. He looked strange. Almost like he was afraid, but mad too.

My chest pulled tightly and I could hear my heart beat in my ear, but I smiled.

"Did you really catch the Holy Ghost?" Madeline draped her arm over my shoulders. I wanted to play hopscotch, but her and Teddy had almost dragged me over to the steps instead.

"She ain't catch no Holy Ghost, she jus ain't know April fools was Monday not Wednesday." Teddy laughed at his own joke.

"You shut up and let her answer. Did you or was you just fakin?"

"I guess it was the Holy Ghost."

"How you get it? I mean what you do?"

"I didn't do anything. I just got it. And then I fell out, No fainted. But not really, because I could still hear what was going on around me, but I couldn't open my eyes to see what was going on. But I could still see stuff. But it was in my head. It was almost like a dream, but it was real or I mean it felt real. Like the people were real." I had not tried to explain it before now. Nobody else had even asked me to explain it.

"Awe man. She is losin it." Teddy made small circles with his pointer finger next to his right temple.

"Either you shut up or you go on somewhere. You just don't know nothing bout the Holy Ghost cause you is the devil hisself." Madeline stood up and got nose-to-nose with Teddy. He looked a little hurt, but not enough to go away, so she sat back down beside me, but she didn't drape her arm around my shoulders.

"How you know it ain't the devil?" Madeline inched a little further away from me and the bell rang for us to go back inside. It was good because the questions had to stop. I gnawed on the inside of my jaw trying to think of something I could give to Madeline to get her back close to me again. I didn't have any gum or candy. I'd worry about making her understand later, but first I had to make sure she still liked me and didn't think I was weird.

We were in the middle of our spelling quiz when Ms. Bayard was called out into the hall. The classroom stayed as quiet as if she were still there. Back at home in Chicago, as soon as the teacher stepped outside, people would be talking and out of their seats and whatever else, but here no one moved and no one said a thing.

A horrible guttural scream came from the hallway. "Aaaaaugh!"

"No! No!" It was bad. Whoever it was, it was bad. I put my pencil down, so that no one could see that my hands were shaking.

Ms. Bayard came back into the classroom. She didn't try to hide the tears streaming down her face. She leaned up against the chalkboard smudging the announcements that she always wrote in the upper right corner.

"Children, we have suffered a tremendous loss." She had said "we." I was a part of this horrible thing because she had said "we." That was what made me start crying.

"Dr. Martin Luther King Jr. was killed last night." Now she was crying loudly. Her body jerking, the tears were pulling her towards the floor. Mrs. Judd, the first grade teacher, rushed into our classroom and pulled Ms. Bayard from the floor. Traces of water in her pressed powder flowed from her eyes to underneath her chin. The two embraced one another, or held one another up.

"What are we going to do now?" Ms. Bayard shook her head from left-to-right over-and-over again. "What are we going to do? It's over! It's over."

Mrs. Judd helped her back out into the hallway. All of the air that was inside the classroom went out with them, and there was nothing left but muffled sniffles, some crying, and a lot of silence. Teddy put his head down on the desk. Madeline folded her arms across her chest and looked up at the ceiling to keep the tears trapped in her eyes. I looked out of the window. The white truck was there to load up the empty barrels that had brought the leftovers from the white school to us for our lunch.

*T*he muscles in my legs burned as I ran. It was so dark that I could hardly see anything in front of me. Gasping for breath, I ran along a tiny trail through a forest. The only things moving were me and the thing that was chasing me. Large trees hung overhead and the dark limbs and vines slapped my face, arms, and bare legs as I struggled to get away. I glanced back and saw a two-headed dragon with large red eyes still coming after me. The dragon, showing his huge sharp teeth, roared and sent forth his forked tongue to capture me. My heart leapt and I tried to run faster, but fell instead. I rolled over onto my back and there he was, standing over me. He dipped his head to devour me. Just as I braced myself for the pain, he let out a huge howl and fell to the ground. Then, I saw someone standing behind the dragon. With both hands holding a *shiny silver sword, her arms were still raised above her head. I tried to get up, so that I could run again, but was paralyzed. This lady frightened me as much as the dragon had. She walked over to me, never lowering the sword. I looked up and realized that the someone was simply a girl, and a small one at that. Surprised, I realized that the girl was me. I scrambled to my feet and stood face-to-face with myself in the dark shadows. We would have been identical were it not for her eyes. Her eyes were those of a savage beast, they were wild and unfeeling. She gave me a broad smile and I realized that her sword shined brightly like it was brand new, but her teeth were covered with blood.*

I sat straight up in my bed and felt my legs. They were aching. I've had this dream before.

"What's the matter with you 'ninnie? Can't you read?"

My whole world stopped and heat rushed from my chest up my neck and into my face. The white boy looked like he was my age or maybe a little older. The red dust on his black tennis shoes matched the red hair that peeked from underneath his white cap. He stood in front of me with a drop of chocolate on his otherwise white apron, stabbing at me with his beautiful green eyes. The blue lettering on the front of his apron matched the letters in the shop's window, COOPERS. A man standing behind the boy, maybe his father or grandfather, laughed and patted him on his back.

"Lady, we don't serve no coloreds here. But you sho is a fine one tho. I bet ah could show you a thing or two. Yessiree" The man had walked back to the counter and was wiping it as he eyed mama. There was venom behind each word and evil in his grin.

"It was a mistake sir. She wondered in before I... You know how kids are." Mama grabbed me by the shoulders and we backed out of the front door. I stepped on her foot almost tripping her. This made the man and the boy laugh loudly.

How could she call him sir? I felt the sting of vomit in my throat. I had wanted a soda from the fountain. She had said that I could get a treat when we first came into town. That's what everyone in Billings calls it, "town." It's really just a block of raggedy old stores, but it's where everyone comes to shop and there's a picture show too.

I wanted to say something to Mama, to ask her why she let him call me a 'ninnie or why she called him sir. When we were two stores away from the soda shop, I looked up at her. She held onto my hand like I was a little girl, but she hadn't said anything. I had to squint to shield my eyes from the sun's bright glare. Her thin lips were pursed and a single tear raced down her cheek. Her back was straight and her chin was high. I couldn't say anything. She was beautiful.

I forgot about the soda until I got home. Then I cried.

"No, Herb it is not okay. Nothing is okay!" I had never heard Mama raise her voice to Father before now. I was happy, no, excited for her. Maybe, she was ready to fight back; ready to become human. I slid out of bed onto the cold floor and crawled over to my bedroom door.

"Bea, you need to calm down. All we have to do…"

"Calm down? Calm down, Herb? These crackers have lost their minds! It was not just me, but Ruthie too. Your own flesh and blood Herbert. This is us! Your own family, Herbert!"

"Did they touch you?"

"They didn't have to touch us. They didn't have to touch us! I know you don't want to get involved and I know you don't care that all the people around here are scared to death…"

"Woman, you don't know what I care about!"

"Herbert, please! It's about the money for you. Damned the people! Damned God!"

I couldn't hear everything that Father said, but I heard Mama clearly. Crouched on the floor, I covered my open mouth. The longer Mama shouted the happier I got. I wondered if she was waving her hands. I wondered if she was pacing, I couldn't tell. I waited for the sound of glass, but it didn't come. I waited to hear Mama beg Father not to hit her anymore, but it didn't come. And when everything got quiet, I quickly crawled back across the floor and into bed. I waited for Father to come talk about how the devil had stopped by, but he didn't come either.

I giggled myself to sleep.

The next evening, the younger preacher came over for dinner. His name was Reverend Tate. He was from Billings, but had been away for a while. Usually, when folks have been "away," they have been locked up in some jail a long way from their family, but not Reverend Tate. He had been to Germany, and to France, and to Jackson, Mississippi. He had been in the army and then, as he said, "in the war that was worse than all the others he'd seen. The one right here on American soil." He had met Stokely Carmicheal, Robert Moses, and Sidney Poitier. These names sounded important when he said them, but I did know any of these people. Father just nodded as Reverend Tate talked. Mother didn't speak and she didn't nod, but she looked at Reverend Tate the same way she looked at Uncle Byrd when he used to talk about the Black Belt and Dr. King and movements.

He kind of reminded me of Uncle Byrd. His deep, brown face was serious, but kind. His tan shirt was heavily starched; he collars and cuffs were crisp. The cuffs of his pants rested neatly on his shining shoes and his cologne was not the heavy, musk of Old Spice. It was light and clean. Deacon Hall came just as we were finishing dinner. They all sat at the table having coffee, even Mama. Father had tried to send her away when he sent me away, but Deacon Hall said, "Naw, we gonna need her too. Yep , we gonna need her." So, she stayed. I tried to listen and even came back down to the kitchen once for water, but I didn't hear much, and I didn't understand what I heard. More and more nights were starting to end this way.

Her daddy got ran out of town by white folks. That's what Madeline had said when we were playing hopscotch during recess. She lowered her voice so that Leanor, who had been sitting on the steps crying, couldn't hear her. I thought about going over to talk to her, but Madeline didn't like Leanor. I'm not sure why, Madeline hadn't given any particular reason. She hardly needed a reason for anything she said or did, she just made a decision and that was it. I pretended to understand what Madeline had said, "Her daddy got ran out of town by white folks," because she said it like it was everyday news and I'd be stupid for asking. Leanor cried all day. Ms. Bayard let her put her head down on the desk and every once-and-awhile she would go over and pat her on the back.

Mama visited some of the women from the church. She was the Women's Missionary Society. She'd started it after some of the "mothers" of the church had blamed her for Father not ever making social calls.

"Ain't right fuh a revun' never to see 'bout his people. If you think our cooking ain't fit for him, then jes let us know." Five of the sisters had crowded around Mama one Sunday after service. I'd lost my space beside her and was pushed outside the circle behind wide, flowered dresses and cheap handbags.

"Of course not, that's not it at all." Mama's voice smiled.

"Then 'zactly what is it?" The same sister who had been talking before, spoke up again.

"Well, Herbert...Reverend Johnson, he has a lot of dietary restrictions. So, he makes sure that I cook at home. I'm sure it is not half as good as yours. Sister Holmes, I've heard about that mean sweet potato pie of yours. I'm dying to try it." Within minutes the group was bragging and laughing. Mama had set days and times to visit some of the sisters in the circle before Deacon Hall came and rescued her.

"Sorry fo' that sister. Sometimes those women folks can get a little put off by some of the simplest things." Deacon Hall held Mama's arm and my hand.

"No need for apologies Deacon."

Deacon Hall opened the door for Mama and then me once we had reached the car. Father was already in the driver's seat with the motor running. When he closed both our doors, he walked around to Father's window. "Some things a woman ought not have to defend herself against Revun." He tried to whisper, but he wasn't any good at it. When he'd made his point with Father, he tipped his felt hat to Mama and then backed away from the window.

From that Sunday on, Mama visited regularly. Now that I was catching the bus to school, these visits were the only times that Father let her drive the car. Every once in a while, he would let her go into town, but that wasn't often.

Sometimes when we visited, she would take food or clothes, or medicine, or all three. She often took paperwork to help them get welfare and commodities. She would read them the information and show them where to sign. Sometimes people just put an 'X' and she would have to print their name underneath. She should've been a nurse. She was good at taking care of people. I always had to go with her, but I couldn't tell anyone about the visits, not even Madeline and Teddy.

"It's nobody's business what goes on in other people's homes, and if I ever hear mention of you telling anyone..." this had become Mama's usual speech whenever we were heading to visit someone, "you better hope that God gets to you before I do." At least it wasn't the devil. I didn't mind not telling. I kind of liked sharing this secret with Mama, just me and her. During visits, I was important too. I held her purse or toted bags while she hugged people or cleaned homes and wounds. That's when I loved her.

It was pitch-dark. I couldn't even see my own hand in front of my face. Mama had turned off of the highway onto a narrow dirt road. Huge trees lined the side of the road that seemed to go on-and-on. At the fork in the road, we went right. We crossed over a cattle-guard that seemed as if it would shake our car apart, then onto another dirt road. Finally, there was a light on a pole in the middle of a yard in front of a small house.

"You mind your manners now Ruthie," Mama said as we were standing on the front porch.

"Evenin'," a tall, lanky, peanutbutter-colored girl opened the screen door and let us inside.

"Good evening," Mama said. "Is Sister McCoy in?"

"Yes ma'am. She up front." Down here, in Billings, up front meant the livingroom, which could really be in the back of the house or on the side. Either way, it was "up front." The girl pointed and then disappeared in the opposite direction. We walked to the back of the small house and there a woman sat at the table with her head leaning against the palm of her hand. An uncovered lightbulb attached to a brown extension cord hung just above her head. Mama walked over and put her arms around the woman. That's when the woman let loose and she cried hard. It seemed like she had been waiting for Mama to come so that she could cry.

After a few minutes, she got up from her seat and wiped her face with a handkerchief.

"I'm so sorry, I ain't mean to bawl like that, it's just..."

"No need for apologies," Mama gave a faint smile.

"Please, have a seat. I'm mighty glad to see ya." The lady pointed to one of the mix-match chairs on the opposite side of the long wood table. Covered with scratches and chips in the wood, the table looked old and worn-out, but it was set nicely. A long white table runner ran neatly down the middle. A glass vase with fresh flowers sat neatly in the center of the table with a butter tray and case knife right beside it. They had fresh flowers. We never had fresh flowers, ever. "'Scuse the mess, I jes ain't been at myself today. Like some coffee? I was jes about to brew a fresh pot."

"That would be nice. Thank you." I handed Mama her purse as she sat down at the table. I felt out of place standing there in the kitchen. There was a loud humming noise coming from the green icebox and I could hear boys' voices coming from the next room. The woman took a box of matches from underneath the sink. Then, she walked over and picked up a piece of paper from the stack that was in the corner.

"I see ya brought ya lil' helper." The woman smiled at me. She could have been pretty once. Her teeth were perfect and straight. She had perfect oval-shaped eyes with full eyelashes. But her full lips were drawn downwards into a permanent frown even when she smiled. Her full face matched her heavy chest and body. She looked tired. "Everleanor!" She yelled and turned the knob on the stove, lit the paper with the match, and stuck it into the eye. There was a windy swooshing sound and then fire. She placed a small handle-less silver pot filled with water onto the stove and came back to sit at the table. "Everleanor!" The second time she yelled, a girl answered and I could tell by the sound of the quick footsteps that she was running towards us from the direction the lanky girl had disappeared.

"Ma'am?" It was Leanor. She stopped when she saw me. She hated me. I could tell by the way she looked at me. Sometimes Madeline called her snot-nose, and I laughed.

"Everleanor, we got company. You make…what's your name darlin'?"

"Ruthie." I almost whispered.

"That's right, you make Rufie feel at home."

"Me, Tootie, and Carolyn in there doin' our homework." Leanor tried to get out of keeping me company. She stood in the opening, where a door had once been. She creased her brow and stared at me like she was put off by my being here. I wanted to tell her that I didn't even want to come, that I had to because I wasn't old enough to stay at home alone yet.

She had on a brown dress with little yellow flowers all over it. The dress had to be two sizes too big, probably her play clothes. Her hair was down, not in the five plaits that she usually wore to school. Leaning against the empty doorframe, Leanor lifted her right foot and scratched the back of her left leg. She was barefoot. Mama never let me walk around the house without any shoes or socks on. "You want to catch a death of pneumonia?" I waited for Mrs. Mccoy to scold Leanor the way Mama always did me, but she didn't. Leanor was skinny and black like me. I stared back at her

"I thought you said you ain't had no schoolwork to do. Ya'll can stay up here in the front so Tootie and Carolyn can finish up they work. Go on now."

Mama and Mrs. McCoy sat at the kitchen table. The front room was separated from the kitchen by a bar with no stools. I was glad that we had to stay close. I would be able to hear what they were talking about.

"Come on." Leanor waved me over to a space on the floor in front of the grass green sofa. The cushions were all sunken in and two of them had huge rips with foam sticking out.

"I was playin' jacks. You can play if you wanna. If you don't that's fine too." Leanor held a bright orange jack ball in her hand. She spraddled her legs. I sat Indian-style and pressed my dress down between my legs so that my underwear wouldn't show. She had lied to her mother about homework to get out of playing with me.

"Sister McCoy."

"Please, call me Margie."

"Margie," Mama started again. "I'm so sorry. There's nothing I can say, but I just wanted you to know that I, the church, will help you in any way we can."

"Yeah, I been meanin' to get to church more often, but it ain't easy with eight chil'ren."

"Don't worry about that right now. All we need to concern ourselves with is you and these children."

"I'm on my twos," Leanor chimed in. She tossed the ball up into the air and swiped her hand across the floor like she was picking up jacks.

"Where the jacks at?" I asked. She looked annoyed by my question.

"They gone. Bubba lost 'em." She said matter-of-factly. "Awe man, I missed. Your turn." I took the ball and tossed the imaginary jacks.

"I'm never gonna get that one without burning your leg." I folded my arms across my chest like I was mad. We smiled.

"Do you have any family here?" Mama asked.

"Naw, I came here with Henry Lee and…," her voice trailed off for a moment. "It's jes me and these kids now. Damned fool! Why he go and hit a white man for?

They gonna kill him. I know they is." She was crying loudly now. Leanor stopped tossing the ball for a moment.

"Don't worry about him." Mama's voice was sweet and strong at the same time.

"Deacon Hall got him out of here a little after midnight last night. He's going to be fine."

"He has peoples in California. So he gonna head that way. He say he'll send for us once he gets settled in up there. But what am I sposed to do til then? What I'm sposed to do?"

"Fours! I'm on my fours now." Leanor smiled and did a little dance with her shoulders. She was nice. I wished I had been nicer to her at school.

"Do you get commodities?" Mama asked.

"No ma'am. Henry Lee always worked. My kids ain't never went hungry." Mrs. McCoy sounded a little stronger now. "I don't even know what he was doing in town. Let lone around Cooper's. He knows for sho' that's a crazy buncha white folks if you ever did see one."

"Cooper's?" Mama asked.

"Yeah, you know that soda shop in town. Henry Lee don't even like no soda and cream makes him sick, but they say he tried to go in there and raise cane," Mrs. McCoy paused for a moment. "But I know good and damned well, sorry sister. But I know Henry Lee ain't tried to set foot inside that place. He hates white folks jes as much or even more than they hates him. 'Specially if they like them Coopers. You know there is some good white folks, but them Coopers sho ain't none of them. They done killed black folks before."

"Didn't the sherriff do anything?" Mama sounded concerned. Mrs. McCoy laughed a mockingly bitter laugh.

"Honey, you aint up nawth no more. Naw you a long ways from there. They say Henry Lee was 'sturbin the peace and tryin' to make 'em serve him and when old man Cooper ask him to leave he haul off and hit him," she giggled a little bit. "Now I ain't gonna say that Henry Lee ain't hit 'em cause he couldn't ever keep a level head, but I know it wasn't cause he was trying to get no ice-cream! They take us all for fools!" Leanor's eyes were glassy with tears.

"No way! You can't cheat me. You got stack jack. It's my turn." I put my hands on my hip and tilted my head to the side, pretending like I had caught her in the act. "Hand 'em over sister." I reached my hand out for the imaginary jacks and ball.

"You got me." We both laughed.

"Sister, I don't even know where to start for getting' no type of government 'sistance." Mrs. McCoy's voice was shaking again.

"Don't worry about anything. I will bring the application back tomorrow and we will get that filled out." Mama was confident. "I just wanted to check on you this evening, but we will get it all taken care of tomorrow. I'll bring some things to tide you over until everything is set."

"I 'preciate that. I really do. 'Nuf of that. How you likin' it down here in the country?" Mrs. McCoy tried to sound lighter.

"Oh, I like it fine."

"Like I said, I ain't made it to church often, but Reverend Johnson sho' can speak. Yes, he's a fine speaker."

"Thank you." Now, Mama's voice was a little softer. She and Mrs. McCoy and somehow changed positions.

"I'm on my sixes," I said when Leanor gave me the ball.

"Ya know," Mrs. McCoy said somberly, "sometimes, Henry Lee…Well, Henry Lee was a good man ya know?" I imagined that Mama nodded her head because Mrs. McCoy kept on talking. "But when we was younger, he'd get full of that liquor down at that cafe and come home and take it all out on me. He'd beat me like I'd stole something." Mama gasped, but Mrs. McCoy kept on talking. "'Til one day, he came stumbling in here ready to whoop me, but I had something for him that day." She giggled a little bit. "He come through that front door and I was standing behind the door with a little wooden bat that we had bought for Henry Jr. the Christmas before. And soon as he got in that door, I started wailin' on him something fierce. He ain't knowed what hit him. And when he was down and couldn't take no more, I told him, next time it wouldn't be so good." She laughed and even Mama laughed a little bit. "He ain't ever hit me again since that day. But 'fore then, you know why I stayed with him?"

Mama stammered, but finally asked, "Why?"

"Cause I love him. That's it, nothing else. Cause I love him. Lord, Lord! Please protect my husband." She was crying again.

Mama was back in charge, "Everything is going to be fine. God is watching over him and you and these children too. It's going to be okay."

"Tens! This is it! You better hope I don't get it!" Leanor and I were both laughing now. She tossed the ball into the air and scooped her hand across the wood floor. She reached out and caught the ball just before it hit the ground a second time and we let out a huge squeal.

"Well, I see you two are having a time." Mama stood above me. "Ruthie, we better be getting now. Thank Everleanor for her hospitality."

I got up from the floor and said a polite thank you. On the way home, all I thought about was coming back on the next day. Then, I would bring my jacks. I had all ten of mine in a small purple velvet bag.

"Can I give Leanor five of my jacks?" I broke the silence.

"May I? Yes, you may." Mama and I rode the rest of the way home in complete silence.

CHAPTER

22

We went to see the voodoo lady. Mama visited Mrs. McCoy almost everyday for two weeks straight. Leanor and I played jacks and laughed like best friends during most of our visits, but we didn't even speak to one another at school.

Over the two weeks of visits, Mama convinced Leanor's mother of a lot of things, like to stop dipping snuff and to stop cursing, but she couldn't convince her that she wasn't hexed. Her husband had been gone for two full weeks and she hadn't heard from him. She'd found out that her second to the oldest daughter was pregnant. And her oldest son, Henry Jr., was messing around with a white girl.

"Bea, I done prayed like you said, but things keep gettin' worse and worse. I gotta protect my family since Henry Lee gone. And this is the only way I know how." Mrs. McCoy's voice was stern. She looked over at Mama who was in the driver's seat of the car, but Mama kept looking forward. Her hands were still on the steering wheel like she was driving. I sat in the middle of the back seat. "You can wait here if you want. You aint got to come in." Mrs. McCoy assured Mama.

"No, I'll come with you." Mama finally took her hands off of the steering wheel. "Jesus protect our souls."

We were parked in the voodoo woman's front yard. It was filled with all sorts of things: a sofa, a car that was missing a hood and all four doors, a stained mattress that had been cut down the middle, a yellowish-brown dog, overturned buckets, a tub, a black goat, a clothesline with dresses and slips and underwear hanging from it, tires, chickens, and even a gas tank like at the filling station. The house was right across the street from our own home. We had never walked across the road to visit the woman who hid behind the green door. Well, not officially. From my window, I'd seen her standing on her front porch. She'd waved, and I ducked down and crawled over to my bed.

"Ruthie, stay close to me," Mama gave me her order without ever looking back.

One Saturday, I had kicked my red, rubber ball across the road. Once I'd gotten into her yard, I kicked the ball closer to the house. It didn't seem like anyone was home, so I took a few liberties.

"Yes ma'am." I answered, but she was already getting out of the car.

We all walked towards the porch. If that was her, she was nothing like I'd imagined. A dainty-looking, yellow-skinned woman sat on the porch with a washtub filled with purple-hull peas at her feet. Her fingers were all purple from shelling the peas. Mama grabbed my hand as we reached the porch. I started up the steps to the house, but Mama pulled me back and we, me, Mama, and Mrs. McCoy, stood at the bottom of the steps and looked up at the voodoo lady. I'd heard about her from kids at school, but I didn't believe she was real. I had heard that she always wore black like a witch and her hair touched her butt when she stood up. I'd also heard that she'd eaten little babies before they were born and killed grown men just by looking at them. Some said she had cured diseases and raised people up from their deathbeds. I couldn't believe that she was real and that I was at her house. From my window, she had always seemed to be a haint – there, but not there. I kicked the rock at my feet. It made a loud clinging sound as it hit the tin that was at the bottom of the house. Mama jerked my arm.

"Ya gonna look at me or ya gonna come?" The lady's voice was deep and gravelly but inviting at the same time. She stood up from her peas and went to the screen door.

"Dun be scared, no. I for you, not against you." She wasn't from here, I could tell. She didn't sound like anyone else in Billings.

"No baby. I from over Louisiana way." She answered my question, but I hadn't asked it aloud. Her eyes smiled as she looked at me knowingly.

Mama and I followed Mrs. McCoy up the steps and into the house behind the voodoo woman. It was dark inside. The curtains covering her windows were heavy enough to keep all sunlight out and all of the darkness in. We walked along a path carved into the clutter of shelves and stacks of paper and furniture. She had lots of dolls, some still in their boxes.

She had all kinds, many that I had never seen before, not even in the department stores in Chicago. I tried to take everything in, but couldn't.

The voodoo woman was small. She wasn't much taller than me and her hair was in cornrows, not hanging down her back. She had on a pink and purple housedress with matching pink slippers. She could've been anybody's grandmother.

The house, despite all of the clutter, smelled like green rubbing alcohol.

"Sit down lady." The voodoo woman motioned for Mama to sit in the chair on the opposite side of the dark mahogany desk where she was now sitting.

"No ma'am. This is for her." Mama sounded and looked like a little girl pointing at Mrs. McCoy.

"Oh, it is for you first daughter. You first. Say you don't believe in me, but you believe in God. All gifts are of God." The woman came from around the desk, pulled another chair over from behind one of the many shelves, and set it beside the one that was already there. She almost looked fragile, but it was clear that she was stronger than anyone in the room. "Now, both you, sit." Mama and Mrs. McCoy sat down. Mama pulled me onto her lap and squeezed. She almost cut off my breath. I was too big for this, I tried to stand, but couldn't get out of Mama's grip. I could not tell if she was protecting me or I her.

"Yeh child. You like me, we da same. You child. You." The lady pointed at me and I stared at her. Her teeth were yellow and she had gray eyes. They were pretty.

"I." I started. Mama smacked my thigh. I'm not like her, I thought, rubbing my stinging leg. People talk about her and laugh at her, not me. I'm not like her. And she doesn't even have any friends. That's because she's crazy and I'm not. My chest tightened and my fist clinched. I'm normal. A little girl. I rolled my eyes at the crazy woman because Mama couldn't see that. The voodoo lady laughed.

"Mrs.," Mrs. McCoy started.

"Abigail. Call me Mother Abigail."

"Mother Abigail. I come here to see about my family. I believe we hexed cause all the stuff seem to be comin' down on us all at the same time."

"Uhm. Yes." We were all quiet as she lit the three candles in the middle of the desk, two white and one red. She looked back and forth between Mrs. McCoy and Mama. "I see you family, but daughter, why you so sad? In your heart." The woman tapped the center of her own chest with her middle finger as she stared past me at Mama.

"I'm not sad, this is for her." Mama let out an impolite sigh and pulled me closer.

"Yes, yes, I see." Mother Abigail talked slowly and ignored Mama's sigh and her words. "You need to bury the child." I jumped at her words.

"Me?" I hadn't meant to say it aloud. Mama slapped my thigh again. I believe it was more from her fear than my disobedience.

"The baby. Bury him out of your heart." The flames of the candles made the voodoo woman's face glow. I felt Mama's chest stop moving against my back.

"My dear, dear daughter. That child separate you and you papa, but only for he love you. Only for he wanted the best for you. You were his baby girl, yes? His only baby. You go wayward, and you try to make up for it now." The woman's face flashed pity, especially her eyes.

I felt Mama's chest begin to move up and down. Heavier and quicker than before, she was breathing.

"Yes, bury the baby. You lose him years ago, even before the little prophet was come into dis old angry world." She smiled a tender smile and nodded her head at me. "But, the boy, he still hold on to you. He beat you down on the inside. I will give you sometin' for you to bury him. Else..." she dropped her head and let her words float off into the air. When she lifted her head again, there were tears forming in her gray eyes. I waited for Mama to send me out of the room or even out of the house so that grown folks could talk, but instead she held me tighter. She was using me as a shield. "And the almost-a-preacher knows. He knows daughter. He knows the son was not his, but was his nephew. He knows and he loves you and he hates you. And that is why he make you lose him. You shame your own papa. So he don't forgive you. No, to his grave. He don't forgive you."

Mrs. McCoy looked at Mama pitifully for a moment, then she reached over and patted her shoulder. Mama pressed her head into my back and I knew that she was crying. I wanted to turn and look at her, not hug her or comfort her, just look. But I couldn't turn away from Mother Abigail. She had said that I was like her and she called me prophet. Ezekial, Daniel, Hosea, those were prophets and they were all in the Bible. I'm not in the Bible, I'm right here. This woman is crazy.

"Daughter," Mother Abigail looked over at Mrs. McCoy, "you husband not dead. No, he fightin' to live. For you and the kids, he fightin' to live. There are no roots on you, just life, daughter, just life. Your son, he be okay. And your daughter will have a good pregnancy and a strong baby boy. He will show you family sometin' new. Yes, he is special." Mrs. McCoy didn't hide her tears like Mama tried to. She wept openly and loudly.

"Tell me little one, am I light or am I darkness?" She was looking at me, speaking to me, but I couldn't answer her at first. Then, I could not keep from answering her.

"Both." I felt strong and I looked her, an adult, straight in the eyes. I knew the answer, but I didn't know how I knew. It was like my dreams, I just knew. "Both."

Mrs. McCoy chitchatted all the way home. She thanked Mama over-and-over again for driving her to see Mother Abigail. She talked about seeing her husband again. She didn't mention her son and the white girl, but she wasn't angry anymore about her daughter's pregnancy. Most of the talking was done by Mrs. McCoy. Mama listened.

"I'm just thankful to God that Henry Lee is okay."

"Yes, yes."

"And Tootie gonna have a boy. Wonder how he gonna make a difference for us. What you think?" Mrs. McCoy didn't give Mama a chance to answer.

"Guess it don't matter right now, just grateful he gonna be healthy. I gotta make Tootie drink plenty of milk. She don't like milk. Ain't liked it since she was born. Have you ever seen a baby don't like milk? That was Tootie for you. And she still don't. Bea, I surely 'preciate this. I do. You know I do."

"Yes, I know."

"I just can't tell you. You been like an angel to me. Surely God sent you to help us out at a time like this. I know you think I'm heathen, but I know God is real. It's just other things is real too. You know now though. Yep, you know for your own self. I thank you though, cause you ain't had to do none of the things you done done for us. Sometimes God will do that though. He'll make people into angels. Who am I to tell you anything bout God?" Mrs. McCoy laughed and Mama tried to laugh too.

I tried not to hear at all. I sat with my nose pressed against the window, looking but not seeing anything. I thought about the voodoo lady's words, but didn't quite know what to do with them. One by one, I shelved them in my mind and pulled them out again, trying to understand what she had meant.

I thought about Cyndi, but knew Madeline and Teddy would be more interested in what had just happened. Cyndi probably wouldn't know what a voodoo lady was anyway, and it would take me too long to try to explain it to her in a letter. I could imagine myself telling Madeline and Teddy that I had been to the voodoo lady's house and that they were wrong. I could see their lifted eyebrows and open mouths while I explained that she wasn't a witch like they had said. She wasn't dressed in all black and she wasn't ugly. She had dolls and pretty pink slippers. I wouldn't let on that I knew that they had not seen her, I'd just say that she must've changed since. But if I told them that I'd been, they would want to know why. I would have to lie. God would forgive me, it would only be a little lie anyway. Maybe I'd say that we were coming from town and found her laying along side the road. So, we picked her up and drove her home. They wouldn't believe that we had been to town in the middle of the week. Maybe, we were out doing missionary work and…but then, they'd ask why we hadn't stopped by either of their houses or why there hadn't been any church announcement about it. I wanted to tell them about the dolls, but I definitely had to leave out the part about me being like her. Every time I thought about it, my heart pumped faster and I got mad all over again. I'm not crazy and I'm not yellow-skinned and people like me. I couldn't tell them that we took Mrs. McCoy either. It was too much to keep straight, so I decided that I wouldn't mention the visit after all. I'd take candy instead.

That night before I went to bed, I prayed. "Please God, don't make me like the voodoo lady. In Jesus name, Amen."

I rode to prayer meeting with Father. Mama couldn't go because she had fresh marks on her face.

"Ruthie, you understand what happened tonight don't you?" Father talked into the rearview mirror, I could see his eyes looking back at me in the back seat. The sweet peppery smell of his Old Spice filled the entire car. He smelled good.

"Yes sir." If a rock could hit him in the back of the head, that would be good. A big rock, but not a brick. I'm not trying to kill him. A small rock, just big enough so he wouldn't go through this speech again, would do.

"I just don't know why your mother acts that way. She always doing things. God has a place for everybody, and you just got to learn how to stay in that place. That's where you're blessed at, in that place." She had ironed his white shirt instead of his blue one. He'd said that she'd done it on purpose, to make him look like a fool, but I'd heard him ask for the white one.

I thought about the baby that needed to be buried. I thought about Mother Abigail. And for some reason, I thought about Uncle Byrd.

"Did you pray for your mother?"

"Yes."

"What?"

"Yes sir," I lied. It didn't count as a lie though. I had prayed for her before, just not tonight. God don't answer prayers about people beating other people up. I hadn't prayed for Carl when I beat him up. Why would I pray for Mama?

"Good. We've got to keep that devil away. Now, if anyone asks about Bea, just tell them that she's not feeling well. You hear? That's the truth. You always tell the truth. She's not feeling well."

"Yes sir."

"The devil may stop by, but he can't stay. Not in our house. Not if we pray. You hear me?"

"Yes sir." It got quiet, so I tried to think of something else to talk about, but I couldn't.

Father started to hum. His voice was deep, smooth, and soothing. It mixed with Old Spice and filled the car. I scooted to the opposite side of the backseat to get out of Father's mirror view. I closed my eyes and rested my head against the seat. Father was all around me. It was warm and nice. I took deep breaths. I didn't miss Mama.

"How 'bout you do an old man a favor and hold this dustpan for me, Ruthie?" Deacon Hall finally gave in to my nagging and let me do something. He always cleaned the sanctuary after everyone had left from prayer meeting, and tonight was no different. Father was in his office, so it was just Deacon Hall and me. Now that he was done with all of the work, he offered me the dustpan.

"Yes sir."

"Let's see here. That grandson of mine can usually find a way to fumble all the dirt back out the pan 'fore he make it to the garbage. Let's see if you can do any better than that." Deacon Hall teased, but I took the challenge seriously. I held the dustpan completely still as he swept the dust and few straps of paper into it. Steadily, I got up from my kneeling position, holding the dustpan in one hand and balancing with the other. I wished I had taken my coat off because it was in the way now, but too late for that. Slowly, I turned in the direction of the trashcan and I walked, one foot in front of the other. A slight wind squeezed through the tiny openings of the closed window and threatened to blow a peppermint candy wrapper out of the dustpan. I stopped moving and let it settle. I held my breath. Then, once again, one foot in front of the other, I inched forward.

"Whoa, that was a close one." Deacon Hall whispered announcing my movements.

"She's off again. Steady, steady now. Is she gonna make it? Looks like she's gonna make it. She made it!" By the time I made it to the trashcan, Deacon Hall was laughing aloud. I flung my arms into the air and jumped up and down once I had completely emptied the dustpan. "Well, declare, you handled that like a pro."

"I do it all the time." I grinned hard and wide. I did do it all the time, but it was never fun like this.

"Oh, I see. Next time, we'll have to move the bin a lil' further back and see how easy you think it is then." Deacon Hall was patting me on the back. "Your dad oughta be done pretty soon. We may as well sit down here, ain't gonna grow no taller." At first it was quiet, I didn't have anything to say, but then I didn't want to stop talking.

"No sir, she wasn't feeling well."

"Yes sir, school is fine. I'm good in math and spelling. I do good in the other stuff too." I didn't want Deacon Hall to think I was dumb in my other classes. "But I like math and spelling the most."

"Yes sir, mama cooked dinner before we came. I had chicken and mashed potatoes. I didn't want green beans."

"Yes sir, I want to be strong, but I didn't want green beans."

"Yes sir, she sick."

"No sir, Teddy don't cut up in school. He good. Some of the other boys are bad. They always want to run and hit, but Teddy, he not like that."

"Mostly, its Madeline and Teddy. That's who I play with most of the time."

"Yes sir, she sick. She get sick a lot."

"Uhm, I like jump roping and hopscotch and redlight/greenlight. I didn't used to be so good at jacks, but I'm pretty good now."

"You played jacks? I didn't know boys played jacks."

"Shoot, I was slicker than anything with some jacks. I had seven sisters you know?" Deacon Hall shook his closed hand and then with a swift throwing motion, released his fist full of imaginary jacks. We both laughed. "Your daddy gonna come out here and get us both for making up so much noise." He looked around like we were in trouble, but I knew Father wouldn't come.

"Yes sir. It's a lot different from Chicago, but I like it here more."

"Yes sir, she sick tonight. She'll probably be better tomorrow."

"Well, sometimes I do. I'll have a dream and it come true or I'll see something, but it's not really there." I regretted it as soon as I said it, but went on when Deacon Hall nodded his head.

"Or sometimes, I'll just know something. Not that I learned it or anybody told me, I just know it."

"Yep, yep. That's special. That's a gift from the Lord. Not everybody got it, but some do." Deacon Hall understood. "Ain't nothin' wrong with that. You just make sure and use if for good. Just tell the truth when it comes to you."

"Yes sir." I nodded my head, not knowing what I was agreeing to, but I thought about the voodoo lady. What is it called when you know someone in your heart? That's how it was with Deacon Hall. I knew him.

"No sir, I hadn't made any mud pies, but Madeline said that we would this summer."

"Oh for sure, for sure. Billings got the best dirt for mud pies." Deacon Hall boasted and then threw his head back and laughed. He was different than other grown folks because he talked and listened too.

"Yes sir, she fine. Well, she was sick, but she might already be better now. She get sick a lot, but not real sick, just a little sick." I looked up into Deacon Hall's face. I searched his cloudy blue eyes that had captured me and wouldn't let me go. I was a deer and he was driving the car headed towards me. Just like I knew him, I knew that he knew me too.

Father took down he picture of White Jesus near our front door and put up a Black Jesus instead.

"Herb, what is that?" Mama asked as Father stood back, admiring the picture?

"What it look like? It's Jesus," he actually smiled and handed me the picture of White Jesus.

"But…" Mama almost started to talk.

"But, what?" Father turned sharply towards her. "But, what?" Mama lowered her eyes and stopped walking towards him. "Beautiful isn't it?" He said to himself. "This is what the scripture says Jesus looks like. Jesus has never been and will never be a white man. When is the last time you heard of a white man doing anything good for somebody else? If he did anything good, there was something in it for him." Father nodded approvingly at his own words. It seems like he was repeating some of the words that Uncle Byrd had tried to tell him over-and-over again. But he had denied it then. Maybe, he was just denying Uncle Byrd.

I liked the Black Jesus. "What do we do with this one?" I asked Father as I held up White Jesus.

"It's trash."

"What about the Lord's Supper? White Jesus in there." I asked Father about the picture that was above our kitchen table. It had been above the kitchen table in Chicago and had followed us to Billings. I never liked it because it seemed like Jesus and the disciples were staring at me whenever I ate, and I didn't like people watching me eat.

"That's trash too."

"But Herb," Mama squeaked.

"Don't tell me those white folks got your mind too...thinking Jesus was white and his disciples were white. Like some white man would ever save something like you." His words were fangs filled with venom sinking into

Mama's creamy skin. I giggled because he had thought Jesus was white all of this time.

"What are we going to put in its place?" Mama asked.

"What? You think I can't get another picture to put there? Why do you always have to ruin everything? Can't a man have peace in his own home? Just take it down like I said."

"No, Herb. I know you can." Mama moved towards the kitchen table. "Maybe we can take a family photo like we've talked about. That would be nice. I…"

"I don't want you and her over my table. I'll get something when I get something." Her? He was talking about me. Her? My name is Ruthie and he would be in the picture too. I looked at him and this time, I had the venom.

"That would be ugly," my voice was deeper than it had ever been before. "And God does not like ugly…like liars and adulterers and fornicators and baby killers." The words were not my own. It wasn't my voice, but they were my eyes, piercing the thin flesh of his neck. Father turned towards me, but he did not move. "I will put this in the trash." It was my voice again and I headed towards the trashcan with White Jesus.

The air got lighter but the summer heat was damp. It made my clothes stick to my body even at night.

School had already been out for three weeks before Ms. Hawkins even called from Chicago. When Mama got off the phone with her, she said something about Ms. Hawkins' ex-boyfriend, Cyndi, and stomach mumps. Cyndi wasn't coming and no, I couldn't go there either.

I had already planned what we would do when she got here. I would teach her how to make mud pies the way that Madeline had shown me. I would show her how to dig to the best, reddest dirt without going down too far and digging to the devil. We would go swimming at the lake and Madeline had said that she would show us how to pick ju-berries. At first, she didn't like the idea of Cyndi coming, but I'd told her that I could have two best friends, and that we could all be best friends. I wasn't really sure that Cyndi wouldn't make fun of her, but I was sure that Madeline could stand her own ground. I didn't know what ju-berries were, but Madeline said it was fun and that they were good.

"You gotta watch out for the thorns, and oh sometimes it be snakes in the bushes cause they like ju-berries too," Madeline had explained the Monday before the last day of school.

"But maybe you can have a birthday party here," Mama had said it before I could start to cry. I stopped missing Cyndi as soon as I really heard what Mama had said. First, I invited Madeline and Teddy and then they helped me chose the other three, since Mama had said I could only have five guests. She said we would have a meal and cake and ice cream, but I could only invite five.

Madeline, Teddy, and I talked about my party every time we saw each other. The party was going to start at noon, but they planned to have Deacon Hall to bring them over a little early because they had never been in the "preacher's house" and they wanted to see what it was like. Neither of them had their own room either, so we decided that each one of them would get a chance to be in my room alone while the other two waited outside. When we knocked on the door, whoever was inside could decide whether or not to let us in, because it was their room. We called it the room game, and I was excited because they were.

On the Saturday morning of my birthday party, I cleaned my room and did everything else that Mama had told me to do. Then, I put on my pink-and-red Sunday dress, my white knee socks, and my black patent leather shoes. Mama combed my hair into two ponytails, one above the other down the center of my head. The plan was that Madeline would be wearing hers the same way. Then, I waited.

"Herb, will you help me take this rug out so I can shake it out real quick?"

"What you need to shake it out for? I don't know why in the hell you having all these little ninnies up in my house any damned way!"

"Herb, it's only five children," Mama spoke softly and knelt down to roll the rug herself. I went to sit in the swing on the front porch.

It had rained earlier in the morning, but that was okay, we could play in my room after we ate. The damp air made the smell of the giant pine trees stronger. I could still hear Mama and Father between the crickety-ckack of the swing's rusting chains against the wood planks holding it up.

"I don't care if it's five or five hundred. Didn't nobody ask me about a party, and I'm tired of you sassing me woman!"

"I'll do it myself, Herb. Never mind, just calm down."

A rabbit darted across the road and into the voodoo lady's yard. That is when I saw her standing in the frame of her green door. From my front porch, she looked larger than she had in person. I felt a warm tugging at my heart and knew that I liked her. It was the same feeling I had for Cyndi and Madeline. She was strong, not like she could lift up a car or anything, but strong, and she knew it. I could see her smiling there in her doorway. I smiled and waved.

"You know she put hexes on people and stuff," Madeline leaned against the pole standing in the middle of what was called the school playground. At some time, a rope and ball had been attached to the pole. We were supposed to be able to stand around the pole with the ball attached to the rope and hit the ball to one another. I think at least four people could play. I never knew what the game is called because I never had a chance to play. There never was a ball or string, so we used the naked pole for other things. Sometimes, it was home-base for hide-and-go-seek or 1-2-3 red light or Simon says. Madeline's lanky arms and legs looked even skinnier against the pole.

"Oooooh voodoo woman, voodoo woman," Carl wiggled his fingers like he was doing magic and circled Madeline on the pole.

"Aw shut up, boy!"

"You shut up, girl!"

"What kind of hexes?" I chimed in. Madeline turned her attention back to me after she swatted at Carl and missed.

"Uhm, you know, like she can make people do stuff," Madeline explained. Carl breathed in like he wanted to say something, but Madeline kept going. "She can even kill people. She pro'bly kills babies and stuff. She got snakes and all kinds of stuff she be using in potions in her house."

"How you know?" Carl finally got his words out.

"Cause I know!"

"You been in her house?" Carl stooped down to draw in the red dirt. "Didn't think so," he said quickly before Madeline had a chance to answer.

"Well, your grandpa…" Madeline was interrupted by Ms. Bayard's high-pitched voice calling from the doorway, "Recess is over! Line up!" I knew that the hard look that Carl shot at Madeline meant that Ms. Bayard had interrupted a secret or grown-folks talk. I'd have to bring up the voodoo lady again later.

"Don't you tell me what to do in my house! Just who do you think you are?" Father's words spewed from the kitchen out onto the porch, and I wondered if the voodoo lady, no, Mother Abigail could hear them. I hadn't seen any snakes in her house. There were dolls.

The thud of Mama falling to the floor was erased my image of the dolls lining the many shelves along Mother Abigail's walls.

Then, it was quiet again. Mother Abigail had turned and went back into the darkness of what I knew was her living room. I tried to spot the rabbit again. I'd lost sight of him.

A loud crash and the sight of Deacon Hall's car in the distance pulled me to my feet and sent me racing through the front door. I didn't stop until I reached the kitchen, and there Mama was huddled in the corner by the sink. Father straddled her on his knees and punched and punched and punched.

My cake was on the table along with the raw chicken and the butcher's knife that Mama had used to cut it up. The chicken lay in the pan, its pink skin covered with flour and tiny speckles of black pepper. I knew there was salt too, but I couldn't see it through the flour's whiteness. Mama hadn't fried it yet because she wanted it to be fresh for the party. She would fry it as we played games. Madeline had asked if there would be music for dancing. I thought about Uncle Byrd and told her about all the records he had, but I didn't answer the question. I didn't want anything to keep her from wanting to come.

"Please Herb," Mama's muffled voice dripped with honey and fear.

I locked my knees and steadied my stance in the kitchen's doorway. "Stop!" I yelled it like she should have. "Stop!"

And I saw the serpent. He turned to look at me while Father kept punching. It was the same serpent I'd seen many times in my dreams. Nothing stopped. The serpent tilted his head to the left and flicked out his tongue. He was proud. His head and body rose stealthily from his coiled tail. And he stabbed me with the daggers in his eyes. Redness filled my chest and got caught in my throat. It was hot. We were alone. It was not dark, and it was not light. It was gray, and it was blue. Gray eyes and blue eyes. Gray eyes. Blue eyes. I clenched my teeth, balled my fist, and I heard, "Both."

CHAPTER

26

I thought the snake was dead as he lay on the linoleum next to Father who was gasping and twisting. Deacon Hall had tried to use his handkerchief to stop the blood coming out of Father's neck, but it just kept gushing out onto the kitchen floor.

I had tried to kill the snake, but I saw him move when Deacon Hall was trying to stop the blood.

"Here, it's still moving," I reached the knife out towards Deacon Hall. I had clinched it so tightly that my hand was beginning to cramp. He looked at me and then at the knife as if he didn't know what to do with it. He should know. He had killed a snake in this very same place. Except, he had cut its head off. I hadn't been strong enough.

Mama was still curled up in the corner with her hands covering her face. I guess she didn't feel Father stop punching her. I wanted to go outside with Madeline and Teddy, but they hadn't come with Deacon Hall. Plus, my pink-and-red dress was covered with warm, snake blood. I wondered what would have happened if they had come and heard Father beating Mama. How could I explain it? That thought made it hard for me to breath, and everything went black.

Mama rushed me to clean up and change clothes. "What about my party?" I asked. The question stopped her hurrying, and she looked at me as if she were afraid that she had forgotten all about my party.

After a fit of starts, she finally said, "We've got to go to the hospital. Your father. Deacon Hall took your father to the hospital. We've got to get there."
I bathed, and she covered her bruises with makeup. I wondered if at the hospital, Father would tell me how it wasn't his fault, how sometimes Mama got out of her place and

pushed him too far. How it was just the devil. I wondered if we would have to pray so that the devil's spirit would have to flee. And when we finished praying, I wondered if he would say, the devil may stop by, but he sure can't stay here.

The hospital was a long, red, brick building. The windows had black shutters around them. There were no ambulances. There were no large signs announcing the such-and-such Presbyterian or Methodist Hospital of Billings. It was just a long, red, brick building. All of the hospitals in Chicago were at least three-stories high. This one was just one.

The sound of rocks crushing underneath the tires as Mama drove into the red, dirt parking lot filled the silent car. She didn't grab my hand, wipe any excess shine off of my face, or fix any part of my clothing as we hurried from the car towards the hospital's entrance. I tried to keep up, but Mama stayed a few steps ahead of me. Deacon Hall spotted us as we walked through the glass door.

"He gone," he was talking to Mama, not me. "I told 'em how the man musta got away befo' I got there," he nodded towards the sheriff over at the counter. Mama breathed in deeply.

"Say they ain't got much to go on, so don't reckon how dey gonna find no 'spects in these parts seein' how we all stick together." He let out a heavy sigh, lowered his head, and shook it from side-to-side. Mama finally let out the breath she'd been holding and a loud yelp along with it.

The sheriff and nurse stared at Mama as she slid to the floor crying, but neither came over to help. I started to cry because Mama was crying. Deacon Hall kneeled down beside her, "Don't worry none, sometimes things like this does happen. But it'll be alright, God willing. I'll help you get your things together and getcha back home to the nawth soon as the revun is buried proper." I don't know if Mama heard because she never said anything back to Deacon Hall. I wanted to say something to him, but he never looked at me.

I moved closer to Mama and tried to hug her, but she swatted me away. So, I stood back and cried.

"That's the least the church can do," Deacon Hall said as he helped Mama off the floor and into a chair. Once he'd gotten her settled into a chair, and sat a cup of water on the floor beside her feet, he put on his hat and left the hospital. I sat in the chair, three chairs down from Mama, crying and waiting for whatever would happen next.

SHA-SHONDA PORTER is a writer, a public speaker, a powerful coach, and a compelling educator. She has proven time and time again that setting goals, focusing one's energy, and persevering produces desired results. She earned a B.A. in Writing and Literature at Burlington College, an M.F.A. in Creative Writing at Goddard College, and a Ph.D. in Interdisciplinary Studies at Union Institute & University.